# Witchy Magic and Me, Maggie

### Cynthia Magriel Wetzler

Published by Saltwater Press, New York
Edited and Designed by Girl Friday Productions
www.girlfridayproductions.com

Summary: Maggie takes on the threats of a grouchy old Cap'n Hatch on Nantucket with the magical help of her Grammy Apple and her little dog, Blissful.

Editorial: Sharon Turner Mulvihill, Amy Sullivan
Cover and Interior Design: Rachel Marek
Cover and Interior Illustrations: Rowan Mahon
Spot illustrations: (bird and lobster): Pixabay, (jellyfish) Yuliya Vasilyeva/Shutterstock, (seashells) Elizaveta Melentyeva/Shutterstock

ISBN (Paperback): 978-0-578-54333-8

Library of Congress Control Number: 2019910584

First Edition
Printed in the United States of America

*To my husband, Garrett,*
*for loving Maggie and me.*

# CONTENTS

# Witchy Magic and Me, Maggie

# Two Maggies

Maggie Greenleaf admired her art teacher beyond imagination. Her teacher sure could draw. Three quick ink strokes on paper, and there was a perfect whale jumping off the page.

Every morning so far this summer, Maggie tucked her art pad and pastels in her bike basket and rode extra fast to the harbor for her outdoor art class, her heart going *thumpity thumpity* with excitement. What cool things would the class draw today? The white sailboats? The busy sandpipers pecking for food in the sand?

Maggie and her teacher had the same first name, but Maggie Greenleaf called her art teacher, who was nineteen and grown-up, Maggie One. She, Maggie Greenleaf, became Maggie Two. Maggie One was big, bulky and comfy-looking. She often wore loose, faded, flowered jeans. So artistic. Maggie One was even preparing for her very own art exhibit at her college in Boston, where she'd be going back for her sophomore year in September.

Maggie One *never* said things like, "Don't make that lighthouse wiggle, Maggie Two. Lighthouses are straight." Instead she said, "Yes! You've put a wiggle in the lighthouse."

And on top of all this wonderfulness, Maggie One had looked at Maggie's drawing of a horse-shoe crab crawling out of the water and had said to Maggie, "You have a whole bunch of talent. You are a real artist." These beautiful words landed in Maggie's imagination, where they lit up her current dream: her dream that *must* come true, please, please, to be accepted into the Nantucket Art Fair for Adults Only.

## CHAPTER 1

# A Witchy Fragrance

A gusty wind blew off the harbor as Maggie handed Mrs. Droop her best and favorite pastel drawing of her little dog, Blissful. Mrs. Droop was chief organizer of the Nantucket Art Fair and had the final say as to who would be accepted and who would not. Maggie felt her fingers begin to shake and quickly pressed her hand against her shorts.

"Say yes, please say yes," Maggie begged under her breath.

The drawing was titled *Blissful Attacking the Crashing Waves*. It had taken Maggie many tries, but she felt she had entirely captured Blissie's spirit. With a few little dashes of her black pastel and a hint of white, she'd caught that look in his eyes that said, "I'm tough. So don't be fooled by my name or because I'm so cute."

Mrs. Droop squinted at the drawing over her glasses, which had slipped down her nose. A seagull suddenly swooped close to the table and added fluster to the tightness in Maggie's stomach. Blissful sat quietly at her feet, one paw on her flip-flop.

Mrs. Droop held Maggie's drawing of Blissful, ears flying and tail dripping, at arm's length. She turned it sideways. She turned it upside down. Maggie dug her fingers into tight fists behind her back.

"I'm afraid not, Maggie," Mrs. Droop said.

*No! It couldn't be over so fast. I have tons more to show her!*

Before losing her courage, Maggie pulled a big bunch of drawings out of her portfolio. "I have more!"

"Well, all right," Mrs. Droop said. "Let's have a glance at these." Her frown lines deepened, but she spread out the drawings on the long table on the wharf in front of the Arts Center cottage.

"Hmm," Mrs. Droop said.

*She's not rushing, at least. But she's not lingering over them either,* Maggie thought. *Toooot!* The loud foghorn from the incoming ferry boomed, and Maggie's nerves took an extra jump.

"I admit, Maggie, these are surprisingly beautiful for a girl your age. How old are you now, ten?" Mrs. Droop puckered her brow.

"I'm nine right now. But I'll be ten soon, in just a few weeks, in September."

"Hmm. You draw with artist pastels, not Crayola crayons."

Maggie hadn't used Crayolas since kindergarten. Crayolas were for babies. But she didn't talk back to Mrs. Droop.

Mrs. Droop pushed her glasses back up her nose. "You know this art fair is for adults only."

Maggie held her breath.

"I'm sorry, Maggie. As I said, the art fair is for adults only." Mrs. Droop gathered up Maggie's drawings and handed them back to her.

Maggie gulped. She bent down and ruffled Blissful on the white patch behind his ears so Mrs. Droop wouldn't see how crushed she was. Tears were starting. She scrunched her eyes and stopped them.

*Poof!* A fragrant scent of honey and lemon peel brushed by Maggie's face. It tickled her nose and felt like a silky breeze on her cheek. She breathed it in. Linden tree flowers. But there were no linden trees here on the wharf.

Could that scent be what she thought it was?
Uh-oh.

Maggie straightened up and tried to keep her expression neutral.

Mrs. Droop sniffed the air. She sneezed. "*Kerchoo!* Sorry, allergies." She sniffed the air again. The lines between her eyes smoothed out, and Maggie saw her frown transform into a lovely smile. "Let me see those again, Maggie." She flipped through the drawings.

Maggie didn't know if she were more nervous about Mrs. Droop or the honey and lemon peel scent.

Because that scent meant only one thing: Grammy Apple. Her witchy Grammy Apple.

Mrs. Droop closed Maggie's portfolio and patted the cover. "I've changed my mind, dear. You're accepted into the Nantucket Art Fair."

"Oh!" She almost kissed Mrs. Droop on the cheek but held back. She forced herself to talk in a calm, grown-up voice. "Thank you so, so much, Mrs. Droop. You won't be sorry." She held on to her portfolio and ran down the wharf toward her bike.

Maggie popped Blissful in his handlebar basket with her portfolio and started to pedal. "Yaaaaay!"

She, Maggie Eva Elizabeth Cottle Greenleaf, was accepted into the big Nantucket Art Fair. For Adults Only. "Except me, Blissie. Yessssss!"

Never mind thinking about Grammy Apple and that sudden poof of honey and lemon peel. She would bring it up later with her mom and dad, even though any mention of Grammy Apple made them squirm and cough.

For now, Maggie would just think about her very own pop-up tent at the fair, surrounded by the adults' tents in the meadow overlooking the ocean. She would definitely hang her three big drawings, a triptych (Maggie's new favorite word) of speckled sandpipers with fat white tummies playing a frantic game of tag. And also, more of Blissie stationed up in the sand dunes, barking at the splash-plop of the waves below.

Oh, but trying not to think about Grammy Apple wasn't working.

Grammy Apple died five years ago, but Maggie remembered her Grammy hugging her and tying a red ribbon around her dark brown ponytail. Maggie remembered the honey and lemon peel scent. And exactly four days ago, she had overheard her parents whisper something astonishing about Grammy Apple. Something positively wondrous and a little scary at the same time.

## CHAPTER 2

# Grammy Apple

Here's what Maggie found out when she heard her parents talking in low voices through their bedroom door, and here's why her parents were mum about Grammy Apple. Ready? Grammy Apple was a witch. An honest-to-goodness witch.

"People in town are still whispering about witches and your mother after all this time," she had heard her father say. "It makes me uncomfortable."

"What can I do about it? She called herself a witch." Her mother sounded helpless.

Over the next few days Maggie tried many times to ask about Grammy Apple. What had she done that was so witchy? What did it mean to be a witch?

She had so many questions! But her parents always managed to change the subject, and she saw that this topic clearly upset them. Nevertheless, the fact remained. There was a real witch in her family! It was thrilling, really. So mysterious. It also made her shiver. What would her friends think?

Maggie knew three important things about her Grammy Apple. One was that she was an artist who painted beautiful wildflowers on Nantucket. The second was that Grammy Apple always smelled like honey and lemon peel, the fragrance of linden tree flowers. And the third was that she left her dog, Blissful, to Maggie. Maggie kept Grammy Apple's note tucked in her treasure box. It said,

Darling Maggie,
    You can always count on Blissful to help you when you need him.

The note sat right next to her best, most perfect scallop shell, tinged pearly pink inside. Whenever she opened her box, wafts of honey and lemon peel escaped, and memories of Grammy Apple flitted through her mind: setting her up with an easel and pots of paint on the beach when she was three, brushing Blissful together, letting Maggie dress up in her long skirt with the stars.

Today was the first time Maggie had smelled Grammy Apple's honey and lemon peel scent without opening her treasure box. Maybe—could it be? Grammy Apple was here now to help her make her dream of showing her paintings in an art show come true. Where people she didn't even know would look at them, maybe really like them. She closed her eyes, envisioned her Grammy Apple and her Grammy's smile full of love for her, and her heart filled up.

She swung her bike onto Orange Street and home. "Blissful, I love Grammy Apple so much, but should I be scared that she was a witch? Were you ever scared that Grammy Apple was a witch?" Blissful twirled his tail in circles, a sign he was particularly happy and not scared.

Maggie slowed her bike. Maybe she just thought she should be scared. Because really, right this minute, she felt more excited than scared. It was, after all, Grammy Apple's honey and lemon peel scent that helped Mrs. Droop see her drawings in a new way, not just as doodles by a kid. Maggie continued to pedal slowly. What if she loved the idea that her Grammy Apple was a witch, no matter what her parents thought? What then?

But a squeaky voice in her head persisted. *Are you kidding me? Witches are nasty things. How could you like that your Grammy was a witch?*

She tried to imagine Grammy Apple cawing and laughing under her breath, stirring up vile potions in a big black kettle and wearing a tall, pointy hat. But she just couldn't put that picture together with her early memories of her Grammy Apple, who snuggled her and showed her how to draw with a big red crayon.

Maggie bumped her bike over the cobblestone driveway of her sea-weathered old house. She leaned her bike against the porch. "Wait," she said out loud. "Wait, wait." Mrs. Droop didn't know she was smelling honey and lemon peel. She thought she had allergies. But Maggie knew exactly where that scent came from. Could this mean . . . oh boy, that she was a witch too? The thought flipped around in her head like a frantic fish out of water. Oooo. What *was* a witch, even?

## CHAPTER 3

# In the Kitchen

Maggie's father owned a restaurant on the main pier. He stared down at Maggie. He was tall even without his high chef's hat.

"Right, Maggie. Mrs. Droop changed her mind just like that because she mysteriously smelled honey and lemon peel. Are you playing the drama queen again?" Her father scowled. "Honey and lemon peel smells changing people's minds? Humph. That sounds like a coo-coo thing to say. Something your Grammy Apple might have come up with. It was your drawings that got you into the art fair, not crazy scents."

*Daddy must really be annoyed with me,* Maggie thought. *He's not cracking his usual jokes. And he never brings up Grammy Apple with me.* She tried to ignore the drama queen comment. It stung a little. No, it stung a lot.

Her father softened for a moment. "But good going, Maggie, for convincing Mrs. Droop. She's a tough one."

Well, at least her father was making a point of saying that her drawings got her into the art fair. *That must mean he thinks they're good,* Maggie thought. But how would she know? He never told her he liked her drawings. Daddy was really confusing a lot of the time.

Maggie saw her mother's lips tighten into a straight line and heard her say very softly, "Oh dear. Grammy Apple is back."

Maggie's mom looked at Maggie's father. "Drama queen is a little harsh, Paul," she said. She put her arm around Maggie and looked into her eyes. "Grammy Apple *did* smell like honey and lemon peel, sweetie, especially when she was trying to do something nice for people." She glared at Maggie's father.

"But it felt magical, Mommy."

Nobody believed her.

"It probably just seems that way," her mother said. Maggie heard an evasive tone in her voice. Her mom cleared her throat, and Maggie saw her straighten her white chef's apron with PASTRY CHEF embroidered on the bib. It was still covered with flour from the last batch of corn muffins she had baked at the restaurant. The muffin smell lingered around her mother. Maggie sniffed it and felt somewhat comforted.

"No offense, Violet," her dad insisted to her mom, "but may I remind you that your mother, Apple, with her lemon whatever scent, was nutsy. Nice, but nutsy. You know people called her a witch and clearly still do." He looked at Maggie. "You don't want people calling you a witch, do you, Maggie? Stop talking about magical scents. No such thing."

Maggie's brother, P. J., grabbed a broom, galloped around the kitchen table and hooted, "Here's your broomstick, Maggie! Ha-ha!"

"Oh, *so* hysterical, P. J." Maggie shot him a killer glance. "Did you *really* just turn eleven, or are you six?"

Maggie looked at her family. "Aren't you all happy about the art fair? You make it sound like I'm weird or something."

Her mother hugged her again and whispered in her ear, "No, no, my sweet pea. You're not at all weird. You're talented. And I'll help you mat your drawings for the art fair." Maggie gave her a weak little smile and quietly gathered up her drawing pad and pastels. She put Blissful in his bike basket and pedaled off to look for interesting places to draw. Drawing always made her feel better.

She would never, ever, tell anyone that she, Maggie Greenleaf, might be a witch like her Grammy Apple. Not even her very best friend, Tasha. It was one thing that Grammy Apple was a witch. But if Maggie were a witch, too, and everyone knew? What would Maggie One think? Would her teacher even want Maggie in her art class? And what about school in September? It would be torture walking into her fifth-grade classroom. Everyone would look at her funny, except maybe Tasha. And worse, Maggie was sure they would make terrible fun of her and play tricks on her. And say mean things that would really hurt, like, "Eeeek! Maggie's skin is turning green. She's a witch! Gross!"

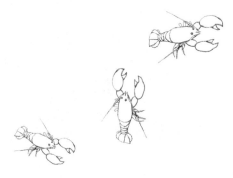

# CHAPTER 4

# Buzz Off

Maggie grabbed her bike, popped Blissful in his handlebar basket and headed over to the pier. She tried so hard to shake off the bad feeling from her father's remark: "You don't want people calling you a witch, do you?"

Why wouldn't her parents just explain to her about Grammy Apple? Why? Grammy Apple was her grandmother, after all.

Maggie turned onto the wharf.

"How about drawing Cap'n Hatch's fishing boat, Blissie?" She always thought the flag Cap'n Hatch flew on his boat was the best flag in the harbor. It was big and white with an image of his yellow lab, Scupper. The dog seemed to move when the flag flapped and fluttered in the wind.

She pedaled faster and couldn't stop thinking about the flag. One thing she knew for sure, nobody else in the art fair would attempt to draw anything on Cap'n Hatch's boat. He was the grouchiest old man on the whole island of Nantucket.

But he had been friends with Grammy Apple. Maybe he would be willing to tell her something about her witchy Grammy. And maybe let Maggie come onboard and draw his flag. Plus anything else that caught her eye.

Cap'n Hatch's boat was tied up to the dock a little distance from the other boats. Something about the way his boat stood aloof in the still water made

Maggie hesitate a moment on the pier. Shadows played across the deck of the boat. It looked so private. She scrunched her eyes and leaned in more closely. What? Cap'n Hatch had painted a new name on the stern for all to see:

## BUZZ OFF

The old name had been bad enough: *Riptide.* She held her breath and knocked on his cabin window.

"Go away! Whoever you are."

She pushed her face against the window. "Cap'n Hatch!"

"Oh, it's you, Maggie." He frowned. "Harrumph. Oh, all right, one second." He got up from his chair in front of his computer. Maggie glanced through the window at his screen and noticed a photo of Scupper with funny marks all over it.

Cap'n Hatch scrunched his white bushy eyebrows together in a big scowl and pointed Maggie to the back of the boat. He came out of his cabin and helped her onboard.

"What's all this?" he said, looking at her art supplies.

*Did he ever stop being a grouchy-face?*

"It's my drawing pad, and you know Blissful, right?"

"Of course I know Blissful," he snapped. "Apple's dog."

"Sorry to bother you, Cap'n Hatch, but I wondered if I could please draw your boat? Especially your flag of Scupper? I'm working on my exhibit for the art fair."

"Hmph. Drawing again, Maggie-girl? I suppose you'll be a famous artist someday."

"I hope so. I'm the youngest person to be accepted in the art fair *ever*. All the rest are grown-ups."

"Well, you can draw the outside of the boat. That's it."

*Old grumpy-puss,* Maggie thought again.

She caught another glimpse of Cap'n Hatch's computer screen through the open cabin door.

"Why does Scupper's picture have funny marks all over it?"

"Harrumph." He leaned in and poked a finger at her face. "No business of yours!" His voice rose, and an apple tattoo on his arm started to wiggle. "Cut that out." He put his hand over the apple tattoo.

Maggie stared at Cap'n Hatch. Had she really just seen his tattoo wiggle?

"Well, if you must know, Miss Nosy-Pants, I can't help bragging about that computer picture of Scupper." He leaned down and whispered in her ear. "Harrumph. It's steganography. That's right, something you know nothing about, Maggie-girl. 'Stego' to those of us in the know." He narrowed his eyes and pulled his backward baseball cap tighter over his gray hair, which curled up around the rim. The cap had a picture of a boat on it. Cap'n Hatch whispered, "I can pass top secret messages in code. Took me a while to get the hang of it."

Maggie whispered back, "What top secret messages?"

"Important communications with someone in Boston, for your information," Cap'n Hatch said. "And it's not for you to find out what! I'm allowed secrets at my age. Eighty-one, you know."

He stepped back. "Now I'm sorry I told you. Don't you dare blab about this with anyone or . . . or I'll tell the whole town, especially your friends, that your Grammy Apple was a witch." His voice boomed like the foghorn on the town ferry.

Maggie shot off the boat, a lit firecracker, clutching both her drawing pad and Blissful, who was yapping and growling at Cap'n Hatch.

Cap'n Hatch shook his finger at her, hard. "Remember, missy. I know your family secret. Your Grammy Apple was a witch. Yes she was!"

Maggie glanced back. She saw shaggy white eyebrows bouncing up and down.

"What's more, I bet you're a witch, Maggie Greenleaf! And I'll tell! What do you think of that? So keep that mouth zipped about the picture of Scupper. And steganography!" He made a gesture with his finger across his mouth, like zipping it.

*Wow. He's not kidding.* Maggie raced back down the narrow pier to her bike. *Mean old man. Well, phooey on him.* When she was farther away, she called out, "I heard my mother tell my father that you asked Grammy Apple to marry you before

Grandpa did." She planted her free hand on her hip. "And she said NO!"

Maybe *that* would stop him from blabbing.

"Well, Miss Mouth. So what." He disappeared back into the cabin.

## CHAPTER 5

# Witchy Magic in the Dune Grasses

Maggie flew to her bike and pedaled really hard through town to her secret ocean cove. She and Tasha were meeting there so Tasha could photograph the little sandpipers skittering across the hard, wet sand by the breaking waves.

A vision of Cap'n Hatch's scary face, bushy white eyebrows popping up and down, flashed in front of her at every turn in the road. She felt a little sick. She got off her bike and dropped it in the dunes.

With Blissful in the lead they plowed through the dune grasses, thick patches of green that reached way over Blissie's head. They ran straight down the dunes to Maggie's driftwood log. She plopped on top of it, where it was as wide and comfortable as her hammock swing at home. Her log was warm from the sun and always felt like a friend, especially today. She looked up at the seagulls swooping around in the blue sky. They were happy she was here on her log, too, she thought.

This cove was Maggie and Blissful's secret happy place. There were no wooden steps leading down the dunes to this tiny ocean inlet. Only the year-rounders knew it existed. Maggie loved that it was so quiet here.

She closed her eyes. The only sound was the *whoosh* and *plop* of the waves breaking over big boulders, an ocean lullaby. She inhaled the briny fragrance wafting in from the sea and scrunched sand between her toes, just like she had done millions of times since she was very little. She felt her insides relax, like a sunbathing jellyfish.

Maggie shaded her eyes with her hand and looked up and down the beach for Tasha. Maggie hoped she would come early. Tasha was the only other person she had told about the cove. Her eyes skimmed over familiar little footprints in the sand, the web-shaped lines made by the darting sandpipers. The web prints looked like three-pronged forks, disappearing into the water's edge and reappearing a little way up the beach. She'd draw them and make them into a design, she thought. Tasha could photograph them.

"I'm so excited about this art fair!" Maggie said to the sandpipers. "Wait till Tasha hears." But how much should she tell her?

Tasha was Maggie's honest and truly best friend since forever, kindergarten actually, and they told each other (almost) everything. Except that Maggie hadn't told her about Grammy Apple being a witch.

But Grammy Apple had helped Maggie get into the art fair, and this information was absolutely too thrilling to keep to herself. Even though she had said she absolutely wouldn't tell a soul about Grammy Apple's witchy magic and that maybe she, Maggie, was also a witch, Maggie was now bursting to tell Tasha everything. She just didn't know what Tasha would say about the witchy part. And she surely couldn't mention the Cap'n Hatch situation.

She didn't dare tell Tasha about Cap'n Hatch's stupid, mysterious stega-whatever secret and how he boomed at her and gave her a mean zip-your-mouth sign. What if he found out? It would be horrifying if he told people she was a witch. Horrifying. She thought again about facing her classmates in the fall and felt her stomach lurch.

Not to mention that her mother and father would be so upset if they knew Cap'n Hatch had threatened to spread rumors about Greenleaf witches. And it would be her fault. And that made her feel terrible.

Besides, if Tasha knew Cap'n Hatch threatened her, she would probably run and tell her mother. And then who else?

Sometimes Maggie thought Tasha was never going to grow out of her baby stage. Really. She still wore bows on her blond pigtails, and she thought all boys were dumb. Maggie had to admit, though, that Tasha sure knew how to take awesome photographs. They looked like paintings, really. She was always pulling her camera out of a special pocket in her backpack to "grab the moment" as she would say. She took photography classes with grown-ups. Tasha was that good.

Tasha would love taking pictures of the dune grasses today, so still and straight.

Maggie settled on her log and opened her drawing pad to a fresh page. She opened her pastel box and smiled. Scanning all those colors at once was always so wonderful. Her medium-green pastel mixed with yellow would be perfect for catching the sunlight dancing across the tops of the grasses. They looked like straight glistening wands.

Without thinking about it she rubbed Blissie's white patch behind his ears. Up he popped onto his hind legs. He stared at the dune grasses without moving, growling softly. Maggie thought it sounded like a purr.

"Blissie. What."

All at once the whole swoop of dune grasses did backbends, complete upside-down U shapes, like arches. Only one or two clumps protested and refused to bend.

Voices whispered, "Hurry up and draw us, Maggie."

*What?*

The voices, carried by a breeze, floated down from—where? The dunes!

"Do you think we can stay like this all day?"

Maggie clapped her hand over her mouth. Oh no. Did *she* make this happen?

Blissful pattered back to Maggie's side and nudged her drawing pad with his nose.

Okay, she thought. Acrobatic dune grasses? She clutched her pastel and drew them doing their backbends as fast as she could, until she had three pages full of beautiful green upside-down arcs dappled with sunshine. For sure she was the first person ever to draw dune grasses doing backbends.

The familiar smell of linden tree flowers, all honey and lemon peel, wafted around her in fragrant puffs.

"Maybe it's a really special thing to be witchy," she said out loud, "because Grammy Apple's fragrance is beginning to make me like the idea of making magic. Blissful seems okay with it." She stopped drawing. "Wait. It's when I rub his white patch that wonderful things happen. Like Mrs. Droop saying yes to the art fair and now the dune grasses posing for me to draw. Blissful? Hmm. He was Grammy Apple's dog. Wait. Is he magic too? Yikes!" Blissful flicked his tail.

"Blissie, come here." They stared into each other's eyes. It felt as if Blissie were saying, "Yes, you're a young witch, but it's a good thing, not a bad thing, silly." And then, was this possible? Blissie seemed to say, "Keep drawing." *Arf! Arf!*

CHAPTER 6

# Seagulls Too?

The dune grasses straightened up, and seconds later Maggie spotted Tasha waving at her from down the beach.

"Blissie, should I tell Tasha about the dune grasses and you? See how she takes it? I absolutely have to. It's too exciting, too wild, too everything! And it has nothing to do with Cap'n Hatch."

She plunged right in, before Tasha even sat down on the log.

"Tasha, what would you say if I told you that those dune grasses did backbends and then straightened up? And, get this. They whispered to me, I swear, to hurry up and draw them. Look what I saw."

She showed Tasha her drawings. "Upside-down U shapes."

"What the heck?" Tasha said. "Backbends? No way."

*I knew it,* Maggie thought. *Tasha's going to think I'm making this up to show off my imagination, or worse, she'll believe me and think I'm really scary.*

Tasha looked at Maggie hard and then burst out, "Maggie, this is awesome!"

Was that really excitement dancing around in Tasha's round blue eyes? Or was Tasha mocking her?

"You mean you really, really saw the dune grasses do backbends all together?"

"Yes, yes, I swear, Tasha!"

"And whisper to you to hurry up and draw them?"

"Yes! And Blissie was part of it too. I rubbed his white patch, and the dune grasses did their backbends."

Tasha sighed. "You're so lucky, Maggie. My mom says she sees magic like that, and I wish I could. I mean, I *really* wish I could. She told me that sometimes wilted roses in her flower shop perk up before her eyes, and antique Nantucket baskets appear from nowhere and settle themselves in her shop window."

"Wow, no way!"

"I didn't tell you because I didn't want you to think my mom was peculiar."

"I would never think your mom was peculiar, Tasha," Maggie said.

Tasha looked at her camera, with all the latest technology. She told Maggie it had been a gift from her father and that he encouraged her to take pictures all over the island. "But so far everything I look at through my camera is pretty regular," Tasha said.

"But, Tasha, really? You think I'm lucky? Not totally weird?"

Tasha closed her eyes. "I dream about seeing magic like my mom. It never happens to me. Imagine what it would be like to take pictures of magical things like acrobatic dune grasses! I'd have pictures like nobody else. I'd be famous."

A baby seagull flew down to the wet sand where the waves were breaking. He faced them straight on. Maggie sketched him as quickly as she could. He would probably swoop off any second. Tasha walked around him snapping pictures.

"Come over here, Blissie," Maggie said. She scruffled his white patch and looked into his eyes. "This is a test, Blissie."

The seagull fixed his black eyes on Blissful and then on Maggie. He sank down on his tummy and did the splits, legs stretched out in opposite directions, something normal seagulls don't do. Maggie stopped drawing.

It had worked.

No doubt about that. She and Blissful had released Grammy Apple's magic, and here was this seagull posing for her. The seagull hopped back up, cocked his little head and stuck one spindly orange leg out to the side. He held it out there straight and sure.

"He's posing!" Maggie stayed very still and sketched this pose, which no other seagull had ever managed, that was for sure.

"Tasha. The seagull, he's posing."

"What do you mean 'posing'?"

"He's sticking out his leg—oh, and now he's doing a cartwheel." Maggie sketched as quickly as she could.

Tasha peered at the seagull. "I don't see any of that. He's just standing there, staring."

"But I see it, for real," Maggie said.

"I believe you, Maggie. You're seeing magic again. I wish, wish, *wish* I could too."

"The thing is, Tasha, there's more," Maggie said in a hushed voice. "My parents won't talk about it, but my Grammy Apple was—are you ready—a *witch*. And now I'm thinking maybe I'm one too. I'm scared. I don't want anyone to know!"

"No, Maggie! It's good! My mom calls herself a witch too. You get to see cool things, like for your drawings. I promise I won't tell."

"Tasha, wow, I was really afraid to tell you about the magic. I thought it might make you think something was wrong with me." Tasha's familiar baby bows in her pigtails comforted Maggie at this moment. "If only I could make it so *you* saw the magic, too, Tasha. You know I would. But it seems like the magic comes through Blissful."

Blissful perked up his ears. "And look at him, Tasha, he's full of himself about it."

*Arf! Arf!* Blissful twirled his tail. He came right up to Maggie's face and twitched his nose. Maggie stared into his round black eyes. Maybe he was announcing to her, "Grammy Apple and I are not the only ones with magic. You have it too."

CHAPTER 7

# Fish Heads and Gumption

P. J. and Maggie liked to take Blissful for romps on the hard-packed sand at Jetties Beach when the tide was low. Blissful flew around like a burst of wind off the ocean, ears straight out to the sides, tail up and pressed flat on his back in alert mode, accosting all the big dogs that paid no attention to him whatsoever. But today, Maggie couldn't enjoy his antics. She was thinking about Cap'n Hatch. She was thinking about Grammy Apple's magical powers and now maybe her magical powers too. Clearly Blissful had magical powers.

"What's the matter, Maggie?" P. J. asked. "You look funny."

*I want to tell P. J. about Cap'n Hatch so much,* she thought. *Cap'n Hatch scares me with his stupid secret, and I don't even know what it is.*

"Uh, nothing, I'm fine," Maggie said.

P. J. handed out a lot of big-brother advice despite the fact that he was only one year and two months older than Maggie. "You don't look so fine." He peered at her and adjusted his glasses. "You look kind of scared. Okay, if you won't tell me, think about this." He thrust out his chin. "Gumption, Maggie. Make sure you have it."

"Gumption?"

"Yes, gumption. Neezer, one of the old local guides at junior naturalist camp, says, 'You have to put your foot in the water, jellyfish or no, if you want to dig for clams.' Gumption, Maggie, gumption. It means to stand up for yourself and be brave even when you're scared."

And Maggie was scared. Later that night, she tossed in her bed and turned her hot pillow over ten times. Gumption. Did she have any?

The next morning Maggie marched right back to Cap'n Hatch's pier to draw other people's boats for the art fair.

Not *Buzz Off*, of course. She didn't have that much gumption.

The long narrow pier looked out on the lazy rolling waters of the harbor, dark gray under a cloudy sky. This pier had the best view for drawing. Sleek white sailboats and rugged fishing craft were anchored to the wharf with names like *Rosy's Smile* and *Come on Board*.

Maggie breathed the seaweed scent that had filled her with contentment since she could remember. She gazed at the distant row of shops, their shingles bleached gray from the salt in the air, giant oak trees fluttering dark green in the breezes and the long blur of more fishing boats down the dock. She was in the middle of a dusky, overcast stillness. She would use her gray pastels.

Maggie wasn't about to give up drawing her harbor just because of a mean old Cap'n Hatch. He sure was flustered when she saw his secret-code picture of Scupper on his computer. His apple tattoo got redder and redder, and he couldn't stop scratching it.

"I hope it never stops itching," Maggie mumbled.

She sat down on the edge of the pier and pulled her drawing pad out of her backpack. She couldn't help sneaking a peek over at Cap'n Hatch's boat, three slips down. All quiet.

"Don't be wimpy, Maggie," she said softly. "Keep focusing on your gumption. You have it. Like P. J. said. You have it because you came here even though you're scared. Especially because you're scared."

She started to draw the masts on a row of sailboats, lined up like marching pencils.

Uh-oh.

There he was. Cap'n Hatch with his baseball cap turned backward, hauling fish off his boat and carrying what? She looked hard. An axe. With a long handle.

Cap'n Hatch threw a fish on a wooden chopping block on the dock by his boat. He raised the axe up high. *Whack!* The axe sliced through the air, and off came the fish's head. Almost. *Whack* again!

He swung around. She froze.

"Watch this, Maggie-girl," he called out. *Whack!* Another poor fish lost its head.

Cap'n Hatch pointed the axe right at her. "Keep your mouth zipped, Maggie Greenleaf. You didn't see anything on my computer! Got it?"

*Grrrrrrrr.* Blissful scrunched flat on his belly, ready to charge at Cap'n Hatch. Maggie grabbed him.

Coming back here was definitely not a good idea.

Ponytail flying, she raced down the pier with Blissie barking his fiercest bark, leaving three of her best color pastels behind. Ouch! She stubbed her toe on the wooden slats of the pier and came out of her flip-flop. She grabbed it. The heck with gumption.

Maggie leaned against her bike, breathing hard. She had better tell P. J. totally everything about what had happened with Cap'n Hatch and about his mysterious computer picture. They really had to stop him from spreading stories about Greenleaf witches. P. J. thought witches were lame, but for sure he wouldn't like the idea of Cap'n Hatch saying mean things about the family to the whole town. She crossed her fingers and scrunched her eyes tight. P. J. just had to listen to her and be shocked into some kind of action.

Maggie biked right over to P. J.'s junior naturalist camp on the harbor and found him crouching by the water's edge. He was studying the underside of a big black horseshoe crab. The other campers were digging up clams, popping them in pails and dumping them in the counselor's roomy backpack.

"P. J., please, it's an emergency. Can I talk to you for a minute alone?"

He looked up. "Maggie? What kind of emergency?"

"Please can we just walk somewhere so no one will hear us?"

P. J. spoke to his counselor, and they headed down the beach.

"P. J., I have to tell you something so scary. And awful. Please believe me. Cap'n Hatch is a maniac."

"A maniac?"

Maggie faced P. J., and the words tumbled out, one on top of the other. "He's hiding something on his computer. It's inside a picture of Scupper. I saw the picture. He yelled at me when I wanted to draw his boat, and he yelled at me in a mean way. He popped his eyebrows up and down; you know how he does. He said the picture on his computer was stega-something. Wait, steg-a-nog-ra-phy."

"Stega-what?"

"Pictures with, get this, secret codes. Then, the *worst* thing, he said if I ever told on him he would tell everyone on Nantucket that Grammy Apple was a bad witch and that maybe everyone in our family is a witch. And that *I'm* a witch. And he took his fingers and made this sign at me, like zip it." She drew her fingers across her mouth.

"Whoa. Slow down, Maggie. That's crazy talk." He pushed his glasses higher on his nose. "There's no such thing as wicked witches."

Maggie noted he was wearing his MR. KNOW-IT-ALL, YOU BET tee shirt.

"Forget about Cap'n Hatch," P. J. said. "He's just a grouch."

Maggie let the "no such thing as witches" remark pass. "But, P. J., listen to this. He waved an axe at me and warned me to keep quiet. It was horrible."

"An axe? Wow. That's different, Maffie."

That made Maggie feel better. Maffie was P. J.'s name for her when he was being big-brotherly.

"He's hiding something for sure," P. J. said.

"Something to do with that stega-whatever," Maggie said.

"I know. I'll ask Ben. He's good at computer stuff. He'll find out about this steganography."

Maggie was impressed P. J. could pronounce it.

Ben was P. J.'s best friend. Maggie always felt herself blushing when he was around. She really liked him.

"Oh, Ben, right," she said, trying to sound casual. "Well, fine. Do you think he even knows how to spell it?"

"Count on it."

# CHAPTER 8

# Chez Paul

Maggie smiled at her dad in his familiar white chef's jacket. They were sipping tall glasses of lemonade at a table on the outdoor terrace behind his restaurant, which overlooked a quiet ocean inlet. Dad smelled like warm cream of tomato soup. Sometimes he was so much fun. He could make a joke about anything, and occasionally he was really funny. Like right now.

"Watch this, Maggie." He hopped up and flailed his arms and legs around, his imitation of a horseshoe crab ambling up the beach.

Except she never knew when his jokes would turn into teases about her. *Please don't let that happen today.* It always made her feel funny about herself when her father called her stuff like "toothpick legs." Like she was skinnier than everybody else. Even though nobody ever told her she had skinny legs. She never answered her father back. She wanted her father to like her and love her, more than anything else in the world.

Once, bubbling with excitement, she had twirled Blissie around and around and had raced outside to the linden tree to draw him. "Simmer down, Maggie," her father had said. "Stop showing off." Not in a joking voice either. In a "there's something annoying about you" voice.

But at this moment they were laughing together at the fluttering little sandpipers, a mama and her little ones, landing *plop* on the seaweed-covered pilings next to their table. The pilings lined the terrace like long fence poles that reached down to the sand under water. Those silly sandpipers couldn't seem to get comfortable on the wooden pilings. They twisted around on their long stick legs, flew away and came back. The mama fixed her beady black eyes on Maggie and her father. *Thank goodness Daddy didn't think to compare my legs to theirs.*

Maggie planned to draw the sandpipers. Then later Mom was going to teach her how to make a perfect velvety custard to use as the creamy layer in their red cherry tarts. So delicious.

Her father didn't notice, or he didn't comment, on Maggie's drawing pad on the table. Or on the different color pastels she had laid out. He folded his arms across his chest and looked hard at Maggie. "I'm glad to hear you're baking with your mom today. You know I'd like to see you spend more time here at the restaurant practicing Mom's baking techniques for her wonderful cakes, cookies and, of course, her tarts."

The restaurant at the end of the pier on Straight Wharf had been in the Greenleaf family for 112 years. Now her father was owner and head chef. It used to be a tavern called Greenleafs, where whaling fishermen came to drink beer after they'd hauled in their catch. Maggie could imagine them all huddled around the bar, probably stinky like their fish. She tried once to draw that picture from her imagination, but it came out terrible.

Now the restaurant was called Chez Paul, after Maggie's father. Everyone loved his lobster rolls and orange-scented stripers caught fresh daily out of the Nantucket waters. And Maggie and P. J. often heard from folks around town, "Your mother's red velvet cupcakes with the cream cheese frosting? Scrumptious."

Here was her father's plan for the restaurant. Maggie would become a pastry chef like her mother and take over her mother's job someday. P. J. would run the restaurant when he grew up.

Her father made it clear—as clear as his glass-bottomed pasta pot—that there were no ifs, ands or buts about this plan. So, many afternoons after morning art class, Maggie spent time with her mother in the restaurant kitchen chopping cranberries for brown-sugar crisps and learning to roll out perfect pastry dough for plum pies and lemon tarts. She loved spending these long hours alone with just her mom, both covered with flour and licking cookie dough from the bowl. Maggie's peppermint brownies turned out so yummy that her dad served them in the restaurant.

P. J. went to junior naturalist camp, except for Saturdays when his father insisted he spend the morning at the restaurant assisting the assistants to the chefs with vegetable rinsing and supervised vegetable chopping. P. J. kept the restaurant pantry in order, too, and organized the pickle jars, bags of flour and tins of spices.

"You kids will make me proud someday. All my recipes will live on through you," her father said. Often.

The only problem was that Maggie wanted to draw and paint pictures, and P. J. wanted to be a naturalist and study the plants and animals of Nantucket. P. J. didn't want to chop carrots. He was much more fascinated by the different species of fish in the restaurant kitchen. He sneaked in moments here and there to ruffle through the pages of his guide to the fish of Nantucket to learn more and more about his beloved fish. He made notes. And Maggie? She couldn't help spending time giving the chefs ideas on how to present the food on the plates in artistic ways. She liked putting little bunches of green basil mixed with parsley next to the fish or steak.

Maggie looked at her father sitting across the table from her on the terrace and picked up one of her pastels. "You know I really love to bake with Mom. When I'm not drawing. Drawing is number one, and baking with Mom is number two. I would never want to miss my morning art classes. We draw something different every day, Daddy, like a school of seals, huge waves at high tide, old anchors washed up on the beach. Stuff like that. It's so much fun."

She heard a distracted "Hmm" from her father. "And my teacher? Her name is Maggie, like me. She lets me draw the way I want to. She says I'm very good." She paused and waited for a response.

He barely nodded. "Is that so?" He didn't even tease her about it. Her stomach lurched in that familiar sickening way it did when she felt small and dismissed by him. She lowered her eyes. If she was nothing much in her father's eyes then maybe she was actually a "nothing-much" girl. She felt like a nothing-much girl a lot of the time around her father.

"Hey!" her father yelled. He peered down the row of tables to the serving station by the rope fence. Two little boys, six or seven, leaned through the rope and grabbed a bunch of red velvet cupcakes off a serving plate while the waitress's back was turned.

"What the heck?" Maggie said. In a split second the boys stuffed the cupcakes into their baseball caps.

"Put those back!" her father shouted. Maggie and her dad darted down the terrace steps to grab the boys.

No one on the left. No one on the right. Gone, down the wharf somewhere.

"Boy, they're fast," her father said.

"They looked exactly alike. Who are they?"

"No idea." He started to laugh. "You have to admit that took guts and quick fingers. Wait till the stomachache kicks in."

"And wait till they try to put their baseball caps on with frosting goo inside!" Maggie said. "Gross."

Her dad chuckled on his way into the restaurant kitchen. Maggie headed back to her drawing pad before she joined her mother and the red cherry tarts. She touched her pastels. Her father hadn't even mentioned the art fair since that day in the kitchen when he had been so disgruntled about Grammy Apple.

# CHAPTER 9

# Corby

"No way!" Maggie said, settling back down at the table on the restaurant terrace to draw. The mama sandpiper and her little ones hadn't budged from the piling near Maggie's table, except now they had all spread their wings and were dancing around on top, staring at her with their little black eyes. It was a miracle they didn't all fall *kerplunk* into the water below. The pilings couldn't be more than ten inches round.

*I wish I could be with you and we could draw together . . .*

What was that?

*The sandpipers will pose for you as long as you need. Don't forget to give them a little bread-crumb treat when you have finished . . .*

"Grammy Apple," Maggie whispered. She whiffed the honey and lemon peel scent.

*Grammy loves that I can draw. What a difference from Daddy.*

*You're ready to do more advanced compositions with your pastels and watercolors. This one could stand out at the art fair. Make sure you draw each leg standing solid on the piling. I luuuuv you. Oh, and talk to Maggie One. She has a story to share with you . . .*

Maggie realized Blissful wasn't with her. So she didn't always need to rub his white patch to bring on Grammy Apple's magic. This time the magic just happened. "Maybe Grammy Apple wants me to really believe the magic can come through me!" she said to herself. "And she wants me to talk to Maggie One about something. What, I wonder?"

A half hour later, Maggie put her finger on the sandpiper's wings in her drawing and made a final gray smudge to emphasize his feathers. She got the feeling somebody was standing behind her, very quietly. She looked up at a little boy, about seven, with dark hair.

"Uh, hi," he said. It was one of the cupcake snatchers. "I came to say I'm sorry." He cast his eyes down to the floor. "Our mother was very mad we took the cupcakes. My brother is inside to say the same thing to the man with the chef's hat." Maggie heard a slight accent. French?

He stared at Maggie's drawing.

"Did you just draw that picture?" he asked. "You're really good."

"Thanks."

"I like to draw, too, but my twin brother, Henri, he likes to be around boats. Not me so much."

"What do you like to draw? And what's your name?"

"Corby. I draw houses, mostly."

"Hi, Corby."

Maggie caught that "I see a house I like and I can't stop myself from drawing it" look on his face. Oh, she knew that feeling. She felt a flash of connection with him. "Well, I'd like to see your drawings sometime, Corby."

His cheeks flushed pink. "Now?"

"Sure. You have something?"

Corby pulled a folded-up drawing out of his pocket. It was a pencil sketch of the bicycle shop by the wharf.

Maggie looked and looked at the drawing. "Wow. This is good. You've drawn every detail of the bikes, the tire rims, the chain links—it's amazing."

Corby's shy little smile burst into a huge grin. "Really? You really like it?"

Maggie nodded yes, yes, yes.

*"Merci!"* Corby said. "Thank you . . ."

"Maggie."

*"Merci*, Maggie."

She had an idea. "I go to outdoor art classes in the mornings. Maybe your mother would let you come too?"

"Wow. You want me to? I'm supposed to go to sailing camp with Henri, but I'll ask."

"Good. Ask your mom. And thanks for saying you're sorry about the cupcakes."

Maggie glanced beyond Corby. She choked. Cap'n Hatch! There he was, heading down the steps toward the restaurant kitchen door with a delivery of fish. He stopped, put his basket down, scrunched his eyes at Maggie and slid his fingers across his lips. *Zip.*

## CHAPTER 10

# Maggie One and Maggie Two Talk

Since Grammy Apple had told Maggie that her art teacher had something to share with her, she needed to figure out how to meet Maggie One outside of art class. This could be really exciting, like Maggie One wanted to show Maggie a hidden bird's nest to draw or something like that. One thing though; Maggie wasn't about to tell her art teacher that the visit was her magical Grammy Apple's idea. Well, she'd just pop over to the ice cream parlor where Maggie One worked and see what happens.

She tied up her bike by the bench outside the ice cream parlor and ran in.

"Hi, Maggie One. Can I please have a dish of chocolate ice cream with coconut flakes before you close?"

"Ice cream before dinner?" Maggie One said. "Yaaaaay! I'll have one too. I'm glad you came by. I have something for you."

They settled on the bench outside the store. Maggie One looked comfy, as always. "Congratulations on getting into the art fair, Maggie." She took a big box of colored pencils out of her beach bag. "These pencils were mine when I was about your age. So some are short. But I loved them. Even put them under my pillow at night."

Maggie couldn't believe that Maggie One wanted her to have pencils she had loved when she was Maggie's age. "Thank you, Maggie One," she said, hugging them to her chest. "These were your special pencils? I'm so happy. Aren't you going to be in the art fair too?"

"No, I'm so busy getting my paintings ready for my exhibit at college. But your family must be very proud of you for getting into the art fair."

"Well, my mom is. Not so sure about my dad."

Maggie One gave her a long, hard look.

"Doesn't your dad like you to draw?"

"I don't know. He never talks about it."

Maggie One took a deep breath. She put her hands on the knees of her flowered jeans and turned toward Maggie. "Can I tell you something? You said in class that you love to ride your bike all over the island looking for things to draw. I can just picture you dropping your bike in the sand, staring out at the lighthouse or the driftwood scattered on the beach. And then pulling out your drawing pad and pastels from your basket and getting lost in your drawing." Maggie One smiled and took Maggie's hand. "Why can I picture this so well? Because I did exactly that at your age." She stopped talking for a few seconds, then looked Maggie straight in the eye and said quietly, "My father would barely glance at my drawings. I remember him turning away. He didn't like that I spent so much time sketching everything.

He wanted me to concentrate on my homework. I almost had to sneak away to draw."

Maggie listened to every word, barely breathing. She opened her eyes wide and didn't blink, still clutching the box of pencils to her chest. "Did you feel bad?" she whispered.

"I was sad sometimes when I was your age."

Maggie couldn't believe her ears. Someone else, Maggie One, who was a real artist, had a father who has made her feel bad too. "Sometimes I think I'm annoying my father," Maggie said in a small voice. Maggie One was the first person she ever told this to. Someone understood?

Maggie One's eyes misted over. She took Maggie's hand. "Oh, Maggie, that's a terrible feeling, I know. But you will have people who believe in you and encourage you in what you love. Listen to them and yourself. Never stop drawing. I didn't."

"I never thought of stopping—ever," Maggie said.

"Of course not! This is who you are! When I was ready to go to college my father wasn't at all pleased that I was going to major in art. He said there were so many artists and so few who succeed. But when my art professors asked me to prepare my own solo exhibit my dad told me he was extremely proud of me. And that he wouldn't miss my exhibit for the world."

Something shifted inside Maggie. She wasn't alone in this experience with her dad. It was an incredible feeling. She gave Maggie One a big hug. Neither of them had touched their ice cream.

## CHAPTER 11

# Steganography and Blushes

Most mornings Maggie's art class met around a weather-beaten rowboat that had washed ashore on the harbor long ago in a winter storm. The boat was stuck firmly in the sand. Green, grassy marshlands dotted the water's edge, home to turtles, butterflies and little snakes. Maggie loved the stillness here. She could just sink into herself and draw. Only the occasional *caw, caaaaaw* of the shorebirds flying overhead broke through the hush on this little stretch of harbor. It was different here from her secret cove on the ocean side with the high, powerful waves. The harbor waves were gentle little *plip-plops*, and it was less secret here.

Maggie One walked slowly around the boat and checked everyone's progress. Her faded, flowery jeans fit right in with the beach-washed colors all around. Maggie caught her eye and gave her a big smile. Maggie One smiled back, winked at her and gave her a thumbs-up. A bond, like a ray of warm sunshine, stretched between them now. Maggie waited her turn for Maggie One to comment on her unfinished lobster drawing. Since her talk with Maggie One on the bench outside the ice cream parlor, Maggie was basking in her new feelings of pride for her passion for drawing and painting. Despite her dad's continued disinterest. It made Maggie really happy to love the artist inside herself, and these feelings settled in her heart like lovely swigs of warm cocoa.

She leaned over to concentrate on Corby's drawing of a seagull. She had brought him along and felt she should take care of him. "Great job, Corby!"

"I'm nervous," he whispered. "Everyone is so much older than me. My brother and I have only been seven for a week." He sat close to Maggie in the stern of the small boat. Some kids in the class brought collapsible seats and were settled on the sand with their drawing pads.

"Never mind them, Corby," Maggie said. "Some are only a few years older than you. They don't even notice you. They're all just concentrating on their own drawings. Go on, do your thing." She gave him a thumbs-up, just like Maggie One had given her.

But Maggie had her own worries. She had broken her promise to the old meanie Cap'n Hatch. She had blurted everything out to P. J., who then told Ben about Cap'n Hatch's computer picture secret. Surely Cap'n Hatch would find out. She just knew it. She swallowed hard and clasped her drawing pad to her chest so tightly it poked her.

"All right, group," Maggie One shouted. "Look at that buoy in the water over there. Forget that it's a marker for boats. Forget that it's red. How do your eyes see it? Not what you think it *should* look like.

But what do you, only you, see? Do you see it flat? Or purple? Draw that!"

"She's tough," Corby whispered.

"But she's right, Corby. Draw what you see," Maggie said.

What *she* saw looming in her mind were chopped-off fish heads, axes with long handles and spooky wisps of gray hair around the rim of a backward baseball cap.

Maggie One came by and stared down at Maggie's lobster drawing. "Don't clutch your pastel so, Maggie Two. You'll choke it!"

P. J. and Ben sprinted up the sandy path toward the old boat, panting. "Hey, Maggie, it's us!" P. J. called out.

"Sorry to interrupt your class, Maggie One," P. J. said, "but may I please speak to Maggie real quick? It's kind of important."

"Sure. Go ahead, Maggie."

Maggie jumped out of the boat. "Be right back, Corby. Just think about your drawing—great seagull so far."

She saw a scared look creep into Corby's eyes and started to turn back to reassure him. But Maggie One quickly leaned over, looked at Corby's seagull and said, "Really nice, Corby, for your first time. Would you like to make his feathers fluff? Draw the bottom line a little heavier. It's good, Corby! Welcome to the class."

Maggie smiled at her teacher. Maggie One sure was a nice person. And Corby's drawing *was* good.

P. J. pulled Maggie toward the water. Out of sight of the art class he said, "Okay, tell her, Ben."

"Okay. So I did some research on my computer, and steganography is a way of sending secret messages back and forth online. You hide the messages in pictures! Awesome or what?"

Maggie was hanging on every word.

Ben cleared his throat. "So it's like a code. No one can understand it or even know what to look for unless you know the code. Get it, Maggie?"

"Sort of."

"Well, listen to this," he whispered. "I'm not saying that Cap'n Hatch *is* one, but steganography is sometimes used by spies."

"Spies? What kind of spies? Spies are dangerous! Wait, is Cap'n Hatch a spy?" Maggie opened her eyes wide and didn't blink or breathe.

"Naw," Ben said. "I was just kidding, really, I promise. Sorry, Maggie."

He took her hand.

*Ben just took my hand. His skin is touching my skin.*

"Don't be scared, Maggie. That was stupid of me. C'mon. I promise I'll help you and P. J. find out what's going on with Cap'n Hatch." He looked into her eyes and grinned.

*He's staring into my eyes!*

Maggie took her hand away. She could barely speak. "'Kay," she mumbled. *Maybe Ben likes me! He seems upset that he upset me. He took my hand!* For one second she forgot about Cap'n Hatch's bushy, scowling eyebrows.

"Cap'n Hatch is just scaring you, Maff, because he's a crabby old grouch," P. J. said. "But steganography sure seems like a far-fetched way to keep a secret, if you ask me. He's afraid of something, that's obvious."

Maggie noticed he made no comment about Ben holding her hand. Sometimes P. J. was very cool.

Ben or no Ben, Maggie couldn't stop picturing Cap'n Hatch passing out leaflets in front of the town hall.

## KNOW THIS!
## GREENLEAFS ARE WITCHES!

"It's okay, Maff. Ben and I will do some snooping around. We're on it." P. J. glanced at the time on his phone. "We have to get back to nature camp," he said. "Don't worry. It's going to be all right, we promise." He and Ben took off down the beach path.

"I'll make sure nothing happens to you, Maggie," Ben called back. He winked at her.

How could he promise that nothing will happen to her? But she gave him a half wave.

Maggie walked back to her art class. She decided right away not to snoop around with P. J. and Ben when they spied on Cap'n Hatch. Cap'n Hatch would have no reason to suspect P. J. or Ben and threaten them with his axe and his zip-your-mouth sign like he did with Maggie.

They just might have a chance to catch him doing something suspicious.

## CHAPTER 12

# P. J. and Ben Are on the Case

P. J. and Ben left their bikes in the parking lot and crept up toward the front window of The Tipsy Rose pub at the edge of town.

"I heard this pub is where the fishermen hang out," P. J. told Ben. "So if we're lucky, Cap'n Hatch comes here maybe."

There were very few cars in the lot, and everything seemed super quiet, like nobody was inside the pub. The hot sun beat down. They were both sweating.

"Stay low," P. J. whispered. "This could be it. Maybe we'll be here just at the right time and catch Cap'n Hatch at something shady."

Ben stumbled on a rock near the entrance to the pub. The rock hit an empty beer can on the sidewalk. *Clank!* Yikes.

"Shh." P. J. crouched and peeked into the window of the old pub, Ben right behind him. A long green pool table took up most of the room. P. J. zeroed in on a plump lady with fluffy gray hair. She sat on a chair and leaned in toward . . . Cap'n Hatch! He was shooting pool by himself.

"Look, Ben. That lady is wearing Cap'n Hatch's baseball cap with the boat on it," P. J. said.

Ben crouched low and peered in the window. "Maybe her head is cold. She's old. Look, Scupper has his head on the lady's lap, eyes closed."

"That's him, all right, Cap'n Hatch," P. J. said. "Dude, duck lower! He's looking over. Uh-oh. Here he comes."

Cap'n Hatch stalked to the door, pool stick in hand. He poked his head out.

"Run, Ben!" P. J. said.

"Could it be that you two shrimps are spying on me?" Cap'n Hatch's white eyebrows went up and down. "Scat, both of you!" He narrowed his eyes and scowled. "Maggie must have told you I had a secret. Too bad for her! You didn't see anybody or anything in here! I'm warning you." He whooshed them off with a swoop of his hands and slammed the pub door shut. *Bang!*

They raced back to their bikes and took off like Atlantic sailfish, the speediest fish in the whole ocean.

"Whoa, Maggie wasn't kidding," Ben said. "He's acting coo-coo and crazy."

## CHAPTER 13

# That Salty Summer Feeling

Maggie's situation was worse than ever. P. J. and Ben hadn't accomplished anything at the pub except to let Cap'n Hatch guess that she had told the boys about his threats.

Maggie hopped on her bike and headed to the beach. She pedaled fast to meet up with Tasha and Jacqueline, their new summer friend from Paris, who happened to be the big sister of Maggie's little drawing pal, Corby. They were going to search for beautiful shells, maybe some small white stones.

Maggie wanted to glue them on wood and build a small birdhouse for her tent at the art fair. It would be like no other birdhouse anyone had ever seen. If she could find seagull feathers, all the better. She'd make a feather roof. Or maybe a seaweed roof. She pedaled faster. Thinking about her art projects and creating them was the only thing that took her mind off Cap'n Hatch and his scowling white eyebrows.

Wasn't it funny, Maggie thought, pedaling along, how she and Tasha had met Jacqueline. Just this morning they were standing in line outside The Country Market deciding between chocolate ice cream with hot fudge or mango-peach cones when a girl behind them who looked their age said with an accent, "I'd go for the mango-peach cone—with lots of sprinkles." Maggie thought right away that Jacqueline dressed super grown-up. She had short straight hair held back with a rolled-up scarf knotted at the side and wore a skirt with lots of ruffles.

"Are you related to Corby? You look a little like him," Maggie said.

"Corby? Yes, he's my little brother, unfortunately, along with Henri. They're twins," Jacqueline said, wrinkling her nose.

"I know Corby!" Maggie said. "He came to my art class with me the other day. He's really good at drawing."

"I know he likes to draw things. But he won't show them to anybody," Jacqueline said. "They're both really pains."

"Really?" Maggie said. "I didn't see that side of him."

"What can I get you girls?" said the boy behind the counter.

"A mango-peach cone, please," Maggie said. "With tons of rainbow sprinkles. Thanks." Tasha and Jacqueline ordered the same.

"Let's sit outside," Maggie said. They laughed and talked together for a really long time on the bench that circled around the big oak tree in front of The Country Market.

"We're here for the summer," Jacqueline said. "We live in Paris, in France. My mom is French, and my dad is American. That's why I speak English and French."

"Can you come to the beach later to collect shells with Maggie and me?" Tasha said.

"Sure! And for seaweed, too, I hope," Jacqueline said. "I'm *cray-zee* about seaweed. Let me check with my mother. I'm sure it will be fine."

When Maggie arrived at the beach Tasha and Jacqueline were already walking near the dunes in beachcomber mode, eyes riveted on the sunlit sand, toes poking for treasures to pop into their fishnet bags. Maggie dropped her bike in the high beach grass, pulled off her flip-flops and ran barefoot down the dunes, her happy feet sinking into the warm sand.

"Hi, Jacqueline. Hey, Tasha," Maggie waved.

All three hugged. "I have a small miracle to report," Jacqueline said. "The twins will be going to sailing camp starting today." She let out a big sigh. "*All* day."

"All day?" Maggie said. "What about Corby coming to art class?"

"I guess he won't be going," Jacqueline said.

"Oh," Maggie said. She felt a twiggle of disappointment. "Too bad. He seemed to really like it."

Jacqueline frowned. "I know Corby is the sensitive one, but believe me, they are both totally annoying most of the time. Listen to this. The other day, when my mother was outside gardening, they locked me in the bathroom. They stacked chairs against the door, and I couldn't budge it. I could hear them belly laughing, especially Henri. Ugh, *si ennuyeux.* Sooo annoying. I mean, they're seven. When are they going to grow up?"

Maggie pictured Corby's eager little face and said, "He was kind of quiet and nice in class. Totally caught up in his drawing."

"Ha, well you don't have to live with both of them," Jacqueline said. She tossed her short dark hair and straightened her coral leather bracelet that had a gold octopus in the center.

*Jacqueline looks so grown-up, like a teenager,* Maggie thought again. *Even though we're the same age.* She glanced at Tasha. She had on her stupid straw hat she had been wearing since the second grade. Tied under her chin! Why doesn't Tasha try to look more . . . more, what was that word? Sophisticated. Like Jacqueline.

"Want to play beach hopscotch?" Tasha asked. She started to hop around the beach.

"That's a baby game, Tasha," Maggie said.

"What do you mean 'baby game'?" Tasha looked hurt.

"Oh, nothing, Tasha, never mind."

Why was she being so impatient with Tasha? With a sinking feeling she realized she didn't want Jacqueline to think she, Maggie, was a baby. Jacqueline was so grown-up looking and lived in Paris where everything must be very *sophisticated.* Maggie felt herself flush. She didn't like herself much right this minute.

She turned away and crouched down to stare at some tiny yellow trumpet flowers. "Look, Tasha, they're growing right out of the sand." Had Tasha noticed she had been a little mean? She really hoped not.

"Here's lots more," Tasha said. "With those funny green leaves like umbrellas. I've always loved these."

*Whew. Tasha's not mad.*

"*C'est un jardin.* It's a garden. A beach garden." Jacqueline said. She touched the soft little flowers and pulled one out of the sand. "Oh! Should I have done that? I wasn't thinking. Sorry. My mom says I do things without thinking."

"Don't worry," Maggie said. "It's only one."

"I'm really sorry." Jacqueline put the flower back into the sand, trying to pat in the roots. "Too bad. These flowers would be pretty glued on the cover of a notebook or something," she said.

"Hey." Tasha swept her arms out in her Tasha way. "Let's do a three-way journal. Want to? We can call it *Salty Summer Feelings.*"

"A secret journal," Maggie said. "Great idea, Tasha! And great title!"

Just then, Corby ran down the dunes, face streaming with tears. He flung his arms around Jacqueline's neck. He noticed Maggie and covered his face with his arms. He sobbed, big violent gulps. "Please, please, Za-Za," he said to Jacqueline. "Don't make me go back to sailing camp."

"Corby! What's the matter?" Jacqueline said.

"I hate it there. I'm, I'm . . . afraid of the water, and the boat rocks, and I don't want to fall out," he said as he clung to his sister. "I want to go to drawing class with her," he said through more tears and gulps, pointing at Maggie.

Jacqueline rubbed his back. "Shh. It's okay. Shh. Where's Henri?"

"He's still there. He likes camp." The sobs slowed down, and he looked at Jacqueline. "Za-Za, is it bad that I don't like camp too?"

Tasha, trying to change the mood, said, "Of course not! Tell me, is your brother your best friend?"

Maggie thought, *Tasha always tries to look on the bright side of things. I should keep remembering this about her. She's special that way.*

Corby said, "Oh, yes, for sure he's my best friend. We do everything together. I just don't always like everything he does. But sometimes it's really fun doing secret stuff together." Maggie saw that Corby was clearly recovering. "We make up a lot of secret stuff."

"Well, come on then," said Maggie. "We all think you can be best friends with your twin brother and have lots of fun together but still not like everything the same."

"Like Maggie and Jacqueline and me. We're not the same." Tasha looked hard at Maggie. "Even though Maggie thinks I'm babyish, she's still my best friend."

## CHAPTER 14

# The Three-Way Journal

The girls put together their new three-way journal. It was Maggie's turn to write in it. She settled with Blissful on the soft green moss under the linden tree in her backyard and traced her fingers around their three names pasted on the cover in gold letters. They all agreed it turned out to be a sensationally beautiful journal.

Jacqueline had arranged the names in a circle. "So nobody comes first," she said.

MAGGIE    TASHA    JACQUELINE

Underneath the circle Tasha had pasted a photo of an eye with a line drawn through it. "Like, PRIVATE. No outsiders," she had said. "I hope people get it. Anyone who finds it by chance, I mean. We should try to keep it with one of us at all times."

Maggie touched Tasha's big glossy photo of the beach garden on the first page and ran her fingers over the yellow trumpet flowers she had painted around the edge. Naturally she didn't pick the real ones to glue on. P. J. would have been furious if he noticed. He got upset when anyone picked any Nantucket native plant. She needed P. J. on her side to continue to help her figure out what to do about horrible old—she didn't even want to say his name.

Maggie was desperate to write in the journal about HIM with the axe and ask her friends for help. But she'd already told P. J. and Ben, and look what happened there. She was keeping so many secrets inside they were giving her a stomachache: Blissful's magical white patch, her newfound ability to make magic happen, Cap'n Hatch's axe and his zip-your-mouth sign. All taboo subjects. And as much as she loved Grammy Apple, Maggie was just not ready to be known as a witch to the whole world. Jacqueline would think she was a crazy person. Maggie wanted to explain in her own way what it meant to her to be a witch like Grammy Apple. When she was ready. At least she knew that Tasha was okay with witches. After all, Tasha said her mom was one. Wow.

Maggie opened the journal. She would just write about Grammy Apple. Maybe Jacqueline would be open-minded about magic if she knew about Grammy Apple.

Jacqueline was so sure of herself, Maggie thought. What if Jacqueline were the one with a Cap'n Hatch problem? She bet Jacqueline wouldn't be scared and would probably march right up to Cap'n Hatch and demand that he stop his nonsense right this minute.

Maggie took her red pen and drew a picture of herself on a fresh page in the journal. She pulled it right out of her imagination. She had on a floppy red hat with a pink rose, and she was holding a shiny red apple.

Under the drawing she wrote,

Grammy Apple
   My Grammy Apple was a magical person. Tasha believes it, too, even though she didn't see Grammy Apple's magic. But listen to this. My Grammy Apple made a seagull do tricks and dune grasses do backbends right in front of my log in the cove. I mean I couldn't see an actual Grammy Apple or anything. But I heard her whisper to me, "Draw, draw, draw, darling Maggie." I was flabbergasted. (Maggie One says this word a lot. It kind of means "shocked.") More proof about Grammy Apple?

Mrs. Droop changed her mind and let me into the art fair when she smelled Grammy Apple's honey and lemon peel scent. Sometimes I can feel my Grammy Apple hovering near me. Not all the time, of course, but a lot. Jacqueline, please don't think I'm a weird person. I feel strong when Grammy Apple whispers to me. But here's the thing. My father calls Grammy Apple a witch. And not in a nice way. He doesn't want anyone to think we are a family of witches.

Love, Maggie Eva Elizabeth Cottle Greenleaf

P.S. Thanks for reading this.

Maggie dropped the journal off at Jacqueline's house. It was Jacqueline's turn to write in it. She was at a swimming lesson. Maggie thought it was a good thing she was learning to swim better. Jacqueline was a terrible swimmer.

Jacqueline's mother said, "I'll put the journal on her bed. I promise not to peek."

The twins ran in through the front door. "Hi, Corby. Hi, Henri," Maggie said. "See you in art class, Corby?"

"Hope so. I mean yes. My mom said okay." He whooped off with Henri.

## CHAPTER 15

# A Nasty Sign

"You won't believe this," Maggie's father said. He was still wearing his white chef's jacket and had rushed home just before five o'clock when the restaurant would open for dinner. Maggie watched him pull a crumpled paper out of his briefcase and smooth it out on the kitchen table. It was a sign.

Don't eat here
they are ~~wichs~~
witches

"What? Oh my goodness. How awful," Maggie's mom said. "Who would have done such a mean thing, Paul?"

"I didn't find it until midmorning. It was tacked to the front gate. I missed it earlier because I went in through the back. Whoever did it must have sneaked the sign up in the middle of the night."

"Oh my. People had all morning to see it. Everyone coming off the ferry."

P. J. stared at the sign and stammered, "Maybe it's someone from another restaurant on the wharf who wants your business?" He avoided looking at Maggie.

Maggie was practically choking with a desperate wish to morph into a seagull and fly out the window right this minute.

*Oh boy. Cap'n Hatch has made his move,* Maggie thought. Shouldn't she just tell her family what she knew? She looked at her dad's exasperated face. No way. Her dad would be so upset and angry with her if he knew she was the cause of the witch sign.

"Or worse," her father continued, "it could be someone in town bringing up the Grammy Apple witch thing again." He glared at the sign and tapped it. "I don't want to think what could happen to business over a silly thing like this. Rumors spread."

Maggie clenched her clammy hands and mumbled, "Excuse me." With Blissie at her heels she ran outside to the linden tree, slid down with her back to the trunk and let the tree prop her up. Do trees love people? Because after this upset in the kitchen she felt noticed by the linden tree. Like it wanted to help her.

"The sign's all my fault, Blissie. What's next? Please don't let it be more trouble at Dad's restaurant." Maggie clutched Blissie to her chest. She felt his heart beating. "I'm scared, Blissie. Really scared."

## CHAPTER 16

# A Mysterious Basket by the Linden Tree

Several days went by. No more restaurant signs. No Cap'n Hatch sightings. P. J. did report to Maggie that he spied Cap'n Hatch lugging a trunk from the ferry. Nothing much to go on there. P. J. also said he was close enough to see the initials *C. J.* on the front of the trunk.

Maggie settled on the velvety green moss under the big linden tree in her backyard and let herself relax against its trunk. Blissful snuggled next to her and helped her prop her drawing pad on her lap with his paw. "I love you more than ever at this moment, tree," Maggie said looking up. The trunk felt warm against her back, and the wide green blanket of leaves seemed to reach down and encircle her. "You help me feel safer and calmer inside, beautiful linden tree."

She hadn't stopped thinking about the witch sign. It was terrifying. But she was determined to continue drawing and adding to her portfolio for the art fair no matter how scared she felt.

A white flower dropped from a high branch into her lap. She heard the tree rustle.

*I'm happy when you are here, Maggie and Blissful . . .*

"Blissie! Did you hear that?" Maggie said in a hushed voice.

*Arrrrf!*

That was a "yes" for sure.

Maggie gazed up into the rustling leaves and lost herself in the swirly patterns. She opened her treasured box of colored pencils, Maggie One's incredible gift to her, and chose a dark green one. She went to work. What came out were little green shapes that might be leaves but at the same time might not. Maggie One said to draw what your eye captures first. And Maggie's eye caught green patches. "This one goes in the art fair for sure, Blissie."

Blissful put his head on Maggie's drawing. Maggie ruffled him all over, white patch included. "Just testing you again, Blissie."

*That's right, Maggie darling. Those green shapes are true Maggie shapes . . .*

It was Grammy Apple's voice. Again!

Then, there was a *whooooosh*, a big waft of honey and lemon peel, and

*Plop*

Maggie jumped up. Oh! A basket. With a wooden cover. Something painted red wiggled around on top. She peered a little closer. It was a bright red apple.

"Blissie, look! Another Grammy Apple surprise, and I'm not even nervous."

Maggie tiptoed toward the basket, squeezed her eyes shut, held her breath and lifted up the lid. The sunlight reflected off dozens of oval mirrors the size of teaspoons. Such a big bunch of them. Maggie sucked in her breath. She touched the mirrors gingerly. They felt warm. She summoned her courage and scooped up a handful, letting them slip through her fingers. She laughed. They glistened so! Little points of fairy light. She tucked one into her jeans pocket. Would it disappear?

This was big. More magical even than sandpipers dancing on a piling or posing seagulls doing cartwheels.

*Whooooosh.* Grammy Apple's scent again. Maggie closed her eyes and breathed in a long, sweet gulp of it before she heard Grammy Apple's hushed voice.

*In less than one month you will
be ten years old, and you are
now ready to see magic.*

*Think of something wonderful
to do with the mirrors.*

*Hint: your imaaaaaaagination
is your magic.*

*Draw everything, my darling
grandchild. I be-lieeeeeve in you.*

*And you will have great
courage even when you are
very frightened. Soon . . .*

"Oh dear, Blissie. It sounds like more scary things
are going to happen. But Grammy Apple thinks I'll
be ready. Let's hope so." Maggie hugged Blissie hard.

"Aren't we lucky to attract magic? If that means
I'm a witch then . . . okay! I'm ready. I really and truly
am. I'll even whisper it out loud. Listen." She took

a breath and gazed deep into Blissie's eyes. "I am a magical witch like my Grammy Apple!"

Then, just what Grammy Apple told her might happen, happened. A beautiful picture popped right into Maggie's imagination, and it was filled with the little mirrors. "Oh, yes, this will be so awesome!" she said to Blissie, who ran like a wild thing over to the toolshed in the corner of the backyard.

*Arf!*

*Arf! Arf!*

Maggie picked up one of the mirrors from the basket and studied her reflection. Had she changed now that she knew she had magical powers and that she was a witch like her Grammy Apple? She looked like she always did. Except not quite. She saw Maggie the artist, not just plain old Maggie.

She wished she could rest her head on Grammy Apple's lap, stay there for a long time and put Grammy's hand on her cheek. She closed her eyes, hugged herself and felt her Grammy as if she were really there.

## CHAPTER 17

# Maggie's Dazzling Idea

*E*ee-yuuuu*—Maggie held her nose. The bags of fertilizer in the toolshed smelled so disgusting. She groped around in her father's toolbox and found the spool of thin, transparent fishing line. Great. Now some garden shears. *Whew.* It sure stunk in here. She pinched her nose shut with one hand and tried snipping the fishing line into short pieces with her other hand. "Oh, never mind the smell, Blissie. It's not bothering you, I see." *Snip, snip.* She cut lots of pieces of fishing line and put them in her jeans pocket. Her project would be . . . amazingly amazing.

The high ladder was buried in the corner of the toolshed. Maggie put her arms around it and tried to pull it away from the wall. "Uhhhhh." So heavy and clunky. Oops! Maggie almost tipped it over. She righted it, dragged it inch by inch out of the shed and across the whole garden to the linden tree.

"Whew." She let out a long gritty grunt and propped the ladder against the tree's wide trunk. She held on tight to the basket of mirrors and made herself go slowly up the steep ladder. It was an old ladder, and the steps sagged a little.

A more complete picture of her project was dancing around inside her head. She would make the whole tree twinkle with the little mirrors. She would call this her fairy-tale tree.

*Arf!*

"Blissful. Stay." She set the basket on the top of the ladder and swept her eyes up into the big tree, gazing all around to choose a good spot to start.

*Arf!*

"No! No barking. You can't come up here."

*Arf, Arf!*

"Blissie. Stay. Guard the area."

On the lookout for anything that moved, Blissful stayed, his head and tail in alert mode. Maggie glanced down at him. Good. Just in case Cap'n Hatch popped out of nowhere while she was up on this very tall ladder. Blissful would nip his leg. Maybe. At least he'd make a ton of noise, and she could escape.

Maggie began with the mirror in her pocket, touching it gingerly at first, just to reassure herself that it was real, that it wouldn't crumble or anything. It was a magical mirror after all. It had a little loop on top, and she threaded a piece of the fishing line through it.

She steadied herself, reached high up into the leafy branches and tied on the first mirror. A sunbeam peeked in.

A few of the younger, smaller leaves began to fight over who would be chosen next. "Over here! No! Me next!"

"Shh." Maggie laughed. "Don't be mirror-grabbers! You'll all have your turn." The little leaves settled down.

She stood on her tiptoes so she could lose herself in the friendliness of these clusters of leaves and strong branches. She stepped up to the next rung of the ladder, deeper into the thick canopy of green. It was like another world up here. Quiet, with rustles.

"Don't forget us," called a clump of old, slightly faded leaves above her head. Maggie honored them with two mirrors tied together—double twinkles.

She tied in more mirrors to her left, her right, above her and below by her knees. Everywhere she could streeeeeetch and, *oof*, bennnnnnd.

She couldn't transport this tree to the art fair, of course, but if it came out right she would make a beautiful tree collage and capture the tiny points of sunlight reflecting off the mirrors with bits of silver foil. The silver foil would be so eye-catching. Yes! Her imagination *was* her magic. Just like Grammy Apple had whispered to her.

Finished. Maggie had been completely immersed in creating her fairy tree and had no idea that a whole hour had gone by. She climbed down the rickety ladder and stepped back.

"Oh, Blissie, just look."

The tree glittered all over with Maggie's mirrors, nearly ninety of them. The breezes twirled them around this way and that. The glitters were so bright that Maggie saw curious little wrens circle the branches in a dizzy dance.

She put her arms around the massive trunk of the old linden tree. In a voice for the tree alone to hear she said, "Thank you for letting me dress you up." Maggie felt her arms ripple. That was a "you're welcome" if she ever felt one.

"Mom, Dad and P. J. won't believe how beautiful my tree is! Right, Blissie? It's absolutely breathtaking!" She hoped her tree might distract her father from thinking too much about the nasty witch sign.

He was bringing home his lobster sliders from the restaurant today, as well as her mom's red velvet cupcakes. P. J. didn't want to miss out on the lobster sliders or the cupcakes and was biking home from camp for lunch.

"What's going on down there?" her father called from an upstairs window. "Lunchtime!"

## CHAPTER 18

# Crushed

P. J. came running across the yard to the linden tree, and their parents followed.

"Hey, Maggie! Wowza! Did you do that?" P. J.'s eyes darted around the sparkling mirrors rustling in the light wind.

"Goodness! It's so beautiful, darling," her mother said. "But where did you get the mirrors?" She glanced down at Grammy Apple's basket and frowned. "That basket has an apple on top." More frowning. "Oh dear."

Maggie heard the distress in her mother's voice and wondered if she should say anything about the magic part of the mirrors. No, she decided. Her mother might be so upset to think that Maggie was a witch like Grammy Apple she would burst into tears. P. J. would humiliate her by telling Ben. And Daddy? He would be sarcastic about the magic part. "Magic mirrors?" he would scoff. Then she could count on him giving her that look that said, "What's wrong with you, Maggie?"

"I just saw the basket sitting there," she mumbled.

"That tree is . . . impressive," her father said.

He liked it. Maggie stared at him. Oh, maybe, just maybe, he would say something special to her, like she was his sparkle girl, full of great ideas, and he was proud of her.

"But I bet those birds are going to poop all over the mirrors." Her father chuckled. Then he laughed out loud, even doubled over with laughter.

Her mother, who was staring at the apple on the basket, turned and said, "Oh, Paul, what a thing to say. Maggie, the tree is absolutely dazzling, darling. I love it."

"No, really, maybe the poops will add to the effect," he said, continuing to chuckle. He was certainly enjoying himself.

"That's not very funny, Dad," P. J. said. He took out his phone and snapped a couple of pictures of Maggie's twinkling tree. "Awesome, Maggie."

"No, it's great." Her father paused. "You know, I bet Daniel, my sous-chef, could do something terrific with this linden tree. He's into art. Maybe you'd like him to come over and add something, Maggie?"

Maggie's heart shrank into a tight, raw ball. It really hurt while it was shrinking. Blissful snuggled his warm little body against her leg.

The tree was a stupid idea. The mirrors looked dumb hanging there. For sure her dad didn't think much of it. She had hoped this time, finally, he would tell her he loved that she could draw anything and make an ordinary tree into a special tree. That would never happen. At this moment it didn't matter much to Maggie that her mother and P. J. were totally taken with her tree.

She managed to mumble in a shaky voice, "I think I'll go feed Blissful. C'mon, Blissie." She folded her arms around herself and walked away as fast as she could. She didn't want anyone to notice the tears dribbling down her cheeks. Out of the corner of her eye she glimpsed her father shrugging his shoulders. She heard him say to her mother, "Did I say something wrong?"

Maggie ran into the house, up the stairs onto the third-floor landing. She climbed through the hatch door in the ceiling and out onto the widow's walk on the roof. It was a small, square fenced-in place. Private.

She threw herself on the hammock.

She was high above the street. She looked out at the harbor and the gentle ebb and flow of the dreamy little waves reaching out to sea. Maggie never tired of their soothing ocean song.

Her dad's chuckles thumped in her ears.

Usually, she loved to imagine the old sea captain, Jeremiah Cottle, up here with her in the widow's walk. Cap'n Cottle built this house on Orange Street in 1739, way back when the ocean around Nantucket was full of whales. She and the captain would stand side by side and gaze out to the harbor, passing his long spyglass back and forth, counting the whaling boats coming back home with a full catch. Cap'n Jeremiah Cottle thought Maggie was a top-notch girl.

Maggie had planned to imagine how he looked and draw him for the art fair, complete with bushy beard and crinkles around his eyes that deepened when he laughed. Since he had lived in 1739, she would put funny brown britches on him. Kind of puffy. She wanted to draw how kind he was. But drawing anything was far from her mind right now.

She sank into the curve of the hammock. Tears dribbled down her face. She pushed her leg against the railing to start the hammock swaying. Maybe she was too touchy, like her father always said.

Footsteps. She dabbed her eyes with her sleeve. *Let it just be P. J.*

The top of P. J.'s head popped through the floor opening. He climbed up and sat down hard on the end of the hammock. Oops! It tipped so high Maggie almost tumbled out. She grabbed the railing to keep from slipping. P. J.'s arms and legs went wild, and Maggie couldn't hold back a good laugh. He grinned at her. Sometimes, not always, P. J. was a super-okay brother.

She giggled as he straightened his glasses. "Okay, okay. So you made me laugh, P. J." They scrambled up and righted the hammock.

"The mirrors in the tree are awesome, Maffie. Don't let Dad get to you. You know he goes for the laugh at all costs."

They plopped back down into the hammock.

"C'mon, Mag, he's okay other than that. Sometimes he's even cool, right? Like when he drives us everywhere? Wakes us up at night to come up here and see a shooting star?"

At breakfast that morning her mom had made stacks of blueberry pancakes. Blissful had stared at her, hoping against hope for a nibble, and the sunlight from the window enveloped the whole family in a warm cocoon. Maggie felt happy, as if she were being hugged. Then her father leaned over to them and said, "Listen to this one, kids. Why did the fisherman throw peanut butter in the ocean?" He choked on his coffee with laughter. Without giving them a chance to guess he said, "To go with the jellyfish. Really funny, right, Pajamas? Right, Toothpick?"

Maggie lowered her eyes. Her legs must be really skinny. Her father joked about them so much. Then P. J. glowered at his father. "You know I hate it when you call me Pajamas, Dad. So please just cut it out."

"Ah, c'mon. What's the matter? Can't take a joke?" her father said.

"Stop trying so hard to be funny," P. J. said.

Her father frowned.

"Oops, sorry, Dad."

"Ah, c'mon, kids. I'm just kidding around. Touchy. Touchy." He looked at them, from one to the other. The lines around his face softened. "I tell you what, you two. I know I joke a lot. That's me. But I sure don't want to hurt you guys. When you hurt, I hurt." His voice grew gentle. "So, when a joke slips out that you don't like, put your finger in your ear and smile. A secret sign. I'll stop right there. I promise. Okay?"

P. J. nodded.

"Remember, finger in your ear and smile," Dad said.

Then,

*Whooooosh*

Maggie smelled Grammy Apple's honey and lemon peel scent waft around her. She felt a surge of courage go through her.

"Teasing," Maggie piped in. "I don't like it when you tease me." Her words came out in quick beats, loud, like the taps of a woodpecker's beak on driftwood. "Like when you call me Skinny Merinks Merandio."

She looked at her father. Did a miracle just happen? He didn't seem that mad.

Now, up in the widow's watch on the roof, P. J. pushed the hammock with his feet, and they started rocking.

"It didn't take Dad long to forget about his promise to stop his stupid jokes," Maggie said. Her father's "poop" words about her mirror tree still really hurt. They were hard to shake. Also, his idea that someone else should come and add to the tree hurt too.

"Dad slipped just now with your tree, Maff," P. J. said. "You have to remember to call him on jokes you don't like." He stuck his finger in his ear and stretched out a smile that showed all his teeth.

"Like he told us to do this morning at breakfast. Remember, Maff?"

Maggie caught his "we're in this together" look. That felt really good.

"It's lame, I know," he added. "But we could try."

Putting her finger in her ear and forcing herself to smile was the last thing Maggie felt like doing. It wouldn't even work.

CHAPTER 19

# Oh No. Another Sign

The next day, since Maggie One had decided to hold art class on the wharf instead of in the washed-up rowboat, Maggie asked Corby if he wanted to meet her before class to draw the outside of the shell shop. They could sit on the bench right across the street from the shop. Maggie knew Corby would love to draw the huge wooden clamshell sign above the door, since he was crazy about drawing buildings. Usually in pencil.

"So I can erase stuff I don't like," he told Maggie.

"You're really getting better and better, Corby. It's wonderful!" Maggie told him. Showing Corby pointers made Maggie realize how much she knew about drawing. Plus it was nice being idolized. She was aware that Corby had a little crush on her. She could feel it when she caught him looking at her kind of moony-like and then quickly burying his face in his drawing.

But she also had the feeling that Corby was struggling inside with something that was upsetting him. And sure enough, after ten more minutes of drawing without talking, Corby looked at her and dropped his eyes. "I don't always think something is fun, and Henri does. Maybe I think it's half fun, and he thinks it's all fun. But he's my brother, so it's probably all fun."

*He feels different,* Maggie thought, *just like I do. And he's sensitive about it, like I am.*

Corby ran home to get the Magic Markers he had forgotten for art class. Maggie lingered in front of the shop. She frowned at her drawing of the shell sign. No good. She had been too busy helping Corby. She put a big *X* through it and ripped it up, but not before she figured out what was wrong. She had smudged her black charcoal pencil too much, and it had created a messy look. "Never mind," she said, looking at her ripped drawing. "If I do ten more, fifteen more, one of them will be just what I want. And if not, on to something else to draw. That's what Maggie One says."

Maggie wandered over to Straight Wharf to organize her pastel box before everybody showed up for class. She chose a spot under the big pear tree that stood tall and sprawled wide above the red brick sidewalk at the beginning of the wharf. The long row of sailboats, roped up to the pilings at the wharf's edge, were bobbing gently in the lapping waves. Maggie felt their rhythm and turned quiet inside, ready to draw pictures of the pear tree or maybe just the shapes in between the branches with the sky peeking through.

She froze.

Another sign.

Right on the pear tree.

Nailed to the tree trunk, kind of low, was . . .

**Another Warning**

Food at Paul's
Restaurant has
witch poison

You could die!!

The thick black letters stared her in the face. Her father's restaurant was down at the end of this very wharf.

"Isn't that silly," said a passerby, nodding at the sign.

"Still," said her companion, "I wouldn't go. If it's the chef's trick to make customers curious, it's going to backfire." They kept walking.

Maggie yanked the sign off the tree and stuffed it in her backpack. Her fingers shook.

"I want to push Cap'n Hatch right off this wharf into the water," she said to the tree. "I hope he'll crack his head hard on a buoy and be knocked out cold. And wake up with a big lump over his eye that will never go away. Ever." She stamped her flip-flop hard on the grass, fighting back tears.

The other kids in her art class began to trickle in, and Maggie took her place at the edge of the wharf. She composed herself. The sign, rumpled and hidden, was polluting her backpack.

Corby ran over and sat next to her. He pulled out a folded drawing of lobsters from his pocket. "That's a good one, Corby," Maggie said, forcing herself to pay attention to her little friend. "Very squiggly and very advanced for your age. No one would guess you were just seven." She looked at him. "But don't fold your drawings!"

She touched her backpack with the nasty sign inside. Another miserable thump of fear hit the inside of her throat.

"Who knows about perspective?" Maggie One said to the class. Maggie tried to focus.

"I do. Kind of," Maggie said. "Things look smaller the farther away they are." Her voice came out raspy and low, full of Cap'n Hatch.

"Do you have a cold?" Maggie One asked. "But great observation, Maggie Two. Here's the thing.

You don't have to draw in perspective. Tell me." She looked over at the big ferryboat that was just pulling into the harbor. "How do you all see that ferry? Like you know it really is? In three dimensions? Or flat in two dimensions?"

Maggie squinted at the ferry. "I see it sort of flat."

"Then draw it that way. All of you. I keep saying this over and over because it's the only way you will find your own drawing style. Do not draw what is in your head. Draw what you see. Three dimensions, two dimensions or upside down."

What Maggie saw was Cap'n Hatch hurrying by not twenty feet from her. He wasn't looking at her or the pear tree at the beginning of the wharf.

Maggie frowned in his direction. *I bet he's going to check to see that his awful sign is still there.*

A man with a striped shirt approached Cap'n Hatch. Maggie recognized him, a fisherman, too, one of Cap'n Hatch's buddies. "Hey there, Hatch," the man shouted. "What's that pretty old heart under your arm?"

Cap'n Hatch was clutching a heart-shaped box, the kind chocolates come in. Maggie could just make out a gold *C* on the front. She turned her face away. *Please don't let him notice me.*

"Nothing! Harrumph. Nothing at all," Cap'n Hatch snapped at the fisherman. "And I don't appreciate your mocking tone." He scurried off down the wharf toward the ferry.

The fisherman laughed and called out, "Is that for a lady friend, Hatch? You got a sweetheart? Ha-ha."

Cap'n Hatch gave the fisherman a murderous look. Then he noticed Maggie. He stopped and scowled so hard his bushy eyebrows came together above the top of his nose.

"Maggie, what's the matter? You look kind of funny," Corby said.

"Nothing, Corby, nothing. It's just Cap'n Hatch. I don't think he likes me or my family."

"Why?" Corby asked. "Does he know you're a witch?"

Maggie's eyes shot open wide. "Why would you say such a thing, Corby? What do you know about witches?"

"Uh, Henri and I read about you and Grammy Apple being witches in Jacqueline's journal."

"You read our journal? Our private, not-for-any-body's-eyes journal?" Maggie hissed at him like a furious water snake. "Corby! That's terrible, and I don't know if I can ever forgive you."

Corby got all squirmy. "I'm sorry, Maggie. I didn't think it was such a big deal. I mean, I don't care if you're a witch, because I know you, and you're nice, really nice. Henri laughs about witches. He calls them evil old wart faces. He says they eat children. Anyway, you don't look like a witch at all." He blushed cherry red. "You're pretty. And it's just pretend, right?"

Maggie didn't answer that.

"And we also saw a witch sign in front of your father's restaurant."

Maggie noticed Corby squirming in his seat. Did he have to go to the bathroom?

He mumbled, "Maybe Cap'n Hatch put up that witch sign. I mean, if he doesn't like your family and stuff?"

Pretty smart for a just-turned-seven-year-old, Maggie thought.

## CHAPTER 20

# The Necklace

Maggie's mother knocked on her bedroom door. "Am I disturbing you, Maggie?"

Maggie and Blissful were stretched out on her bed. She was reading an article, "How to Set Up Your Booth for an Art Fair." Blissful rested his head on the open magazine, making it awkward for Maggie to turn pages.

"Hi, honey." Her mom sat on the bed and took her hand. Maggie saw an "I feel bad about something" look on her mother's face.

"I just want you to know that I think the mirrors in the tree are very beautiful. And I'm not the only one. Mrs. Ginger from next door called me. She said she looked over her backyard fence, and the mirrors took her breath away. She said she can't wait to see your drawings at the art fair."

"That's really nice of her," Maggie said. Though it didn't make her feel any better about her father's bird-poop comments.

"And, Maggie, your father thinks so too. He just lets his jokes take over sometimes." She pulled Maggie into a big hug. "He loves you very much, darling."

"Good," Maggie said in a soft voice. "Because sometimes I feel like when he teases me he doesn't care that it hurts my feelings."

"No, no, darling. Of course he cares. Don't you know that?" Her mother caressed her cheek. "You're his precious Maggie-girl."

"He never says that to me. You may say so, but he doesn't." Maggie was fighting tears.

"Aw, sweetie, come here." Her mother held her tight. Maggie sensed her mother was fighting tears too.

"Your father's a little upset about the witch signs. We can't figure out who would do such a thing and why."

Maggie stopped breathing. If only she could just blurt out, "It's Cap'n Hatch, Mommy. Cap'n Hatch is putting up the signs." But his scowling, bushy eyebrows and his zip-your-mouth sign loomed large in her mind. Worse, she again imagined kids snickering at her behind her back in school this September or taunting her with black cats. She said nothing.

"But on the happy side," her mother said, "I can see that Grammy Apple's magic is bringing you lots of ideas for the art fair."

*She's talking about Grammy Apple's magic. And she never did before,* Maggie thought.

"And you can see her magic. I never could," her mother said.

"Then you're not angry with me, Mommy, because I can see her magic?"

Before her mother could answer, they both heard a rustle on Maggie's dressing table. They hopped off the bed. A golden necklace with a linden tree charm glimmered up at them.

"How on earth did *that* get there?" her mother said.

The linden tree charm had tiny yellow diamond flowers on it.

"What is that?" Maggie asked. She leaned down and peered closer at the golden necklace. She touched it very gently. Funny, how nice and warm it made her feel inside. Blissful was staring at it, too, wagging his tail.

"It belonged to your Grammy Apple. She always wore it. Goodness, that brings back unpleasant feelings." Her mother didn't take her eyes off the necklace. "It was supposed to be mine after Grammy Apple died. I'm one hundred percent sure I packed it away in her trunk in the back attic. I never wanted it. In fact, I hated it."

"You hated it?"

Maggie's mother sat down on the bed and plumped up the pillows. She patted the spot beside her, and she and Maggie stretched out. Her mother sighed. "This may be a sign that I ought to tell you about your Grammy Apple. Heaven knows I wouldn't put it past her to have put it there for that very reason. That basket of mirrors with the apple on top? The acrobatic seagull who posed for you? Her doings for sure."

Maggie knew that, of course, but she wanted so badly for her mother to continue that she kept mum.

"Your Grammy Apple did magical things when she was alive, so why not now?"

"Like what?"

"She could make things happen. When I was five I was stung by a jellyfish—"

"A jellyfish? Yikes."

"Yes. I was running on the beach and stepped on a dead one. He was buried under the sand. There was still some venom in his tentacles, and I got a really bad sting on my big toe."

"Poor you, Mommy."

"My toe swelled up red and itched horribly. Well, your Grammy Apple held me tight, closed her eyes and said something under her breath. The next second Dr. Winthrop appeared out of nowhere and tended to me."

"He just came?

"Yes. The beach was empty, and then there he was."

"Wow."

"So here's what it was, Maggie. Grammy Apple was a magical person. But many people called her a witch, and she also called herself a witch. A good witch." Her mother sighed again. "When I was your age I wished so much that she was like all the other mothers. Normal. And that she didn't wear odd, shiny clothes that looked old-fashioned. The other kids tormented me about her. I can still hear them. 'Is your mother the Wicked Witch of the West or something? Creeeeepy.' Or, 'Tell your weird mother to go back to *The Wizard of Oz*.' Or, 'Where's your gross black cauldron filled with wormy witches' brew?' Stuff like that and worse. Some kids avoided me like I was evil. They snickered when I passed them in the hall. Some parents wouldn't let their children play with me."

Maggie heard the hurt in her mother's voice. It made her sad for her mom. But at the same time Maggie felt extra close to her. *These are my worries too,* Maggie thought.

"Grammy Apple tried telling me about her world in gentle ways. But I closed my ears when she talked about her magical bond with shorebirds and the winds swirling off the ocean. I wanted her to talk about regular things like bike rides or digging for clams with your grandpa."

Maggie took a deep breath. Now was the time to tell. "I can feel what Grammy Apple felt too," she said in a quiet voice. "Really strong sometimes. Like with the linden tree. It's like the tree lets me know how it feels."

A long silence filled the room. Her mother didn't speak.

*Will she feel funny about me now?* Maggie thought.

Her mother put her hand on Maggie's cheek and said in a gentle voice, "I'm glad for you, my precious girl. Really. Not many can feel that. It's a beautiful gift to you from your Grammy Apple. The linden tree was her special place too." Maggie heard oceans of love in her mother's voice.

"Then it's okay if I'm a witch too?" Maggie's heart fluttered hard against her chest. "Because I want to be proud of it."

"Yes, yes, of course it's okay. It's who you are, darling Maggie, and I love every magical part of you. But the witch signs have brought back all those bad memories of being teased about Grammy Apple. They don't hurt me now. I'm a grown-up. But I've been very afraid these new witchy-doings might hurt you."

Maggie snuggled closer to her mother. "The magic makes me feel stronger, Mommy, not scared."

"I wish I had tried to understand your Grammy Apple. I pushed her away all the time. I must have made her very unhappy. Grammy Apple was a wonderful artist, and she spent hours with you pasting little shapes of colored tissue on paper, helping you to paint with watercolors. She would be happy that you love to draw and super proud you are in the adults' art fair."

"Did she have brown eyes with amber glints like you and me?" Maggie asked.

"Yes, she did. All three of us have brown eyes with amber glints."

*Whooooosh*

Honey and lemon peel.

"Mmm." They both sniffed.

"Just close your eyes, Mommy. Grammy Apple will make us both love her magic. And now mine."

A rustle. They looked over at the dressing table. "The linden tree necklace is gone," Maggie said.

"It's back up in her trunk, I bet." Her mother smiled. "For now."

CHAPTER 21

# Seashells and Shame

Maggie made plans with Jacqueline to meet at the Seashell Shop so Jacqueline could give her the journal. Maggie wanted to paste one of Tasha's photos, a small selfie of the three of them by the ocean, on the inside cover where Maggie had painted blue waves in watercolors. Tasha was headed down to the bay beach to take pictures of kids digging for clams.

Maggie was very worried about meeting up with Jacqueline. She obviously had read Maggie's journal entry about Grammy Apple and family witches.

That's why she chose the Seashell Shop, a place where she loved to mosey around and where she felt at home. The old shop had been on the wharf ever since Maggie could remember. It smelled like the harbor, kind of fishy and wet, and she loved the crowded feel of it. There must be thousands of shells here, all sorted in little boxes.

Jacqueline flounced into the shop with her polished fingernails, bright blue, like straight from the beauty parlor. She gave Maggie a kiss on each cheek. "It's how we say 'hello' in Paris." She giggled and gave Maggie the journal. Maggie put it in her backpack and stared at Jacqueline.

"What?" Jacqueline said.

"Did you read my journal entry?"

"Yes."

"And?"

"And I didn't believe you at first. I mean— witches?" She rolled her eyes. "But I talked to Tasha about it for a really long time, and I'm okay with it. Especially the magic part. Seeing magical seagulls is kind of *sensationnel*. Sensational."

*Whew*, Maggie thought.

"Tasha and I had such a good talk. We got close. Like best friends."

"Oh, really?" Maggie tried to sound normal, not jealous. "Well good," she said in a quiet voice. In her mind she pictured her best friend Tasha walking off arm in arm with Jacqueline and leaving her out. Maggie felt her cheeks flush. She dropped her head and zeroed in on boxes of fragile gold jingle shells, snail shells that looked like boats and large scallop shells all purple inside.

"Oh, I love these," Jacqueline said. She picked up a handful of little white clamshells. "My favorites."

"Me too. Definitely my favorites also," Maggie said, forcing her voice to come out cheery. She checked out the small scarf tied around Jacqueline's neck. Jacqueline always wore scarves. Sometimes she twisted one to look like a necklace. So fashionable. Maggie pictured herself wearing a scarf. She pulled the elastic from her ponytail and shook out her long dark hair.

"If Tasha were here she would probably knock over the boxes of shells. She's such a silly klutz," Maggie said.

Jacqueline shot her a funny glance. "You think so?"

Maggie lowered her voice and leaned toward Jacqueline. "Seriously," Maggie said. "I think she's babyish sometimes, and she can't sit still."

The words plopped right out of Maggie's mouth before she could stop them. She clapped her hand on her lips. Oh no, she had done it again. Said mean things about Tasha. What was *wrong* with her? Her breakfast rose up in her throat. She swallowed it back down. "I mean, I didn't actually mean it the way it sounded. Tasha's awesome."

How could she ever, ever say such cruel things about Tasha? Her cheeks flamed hot. Tasha. They were the only two people in the world who saw their teacher, Miss Wolfski, kissing Principal Roth in the dunes! What a stupid thing to think of right this moment. But she and Tasha had had hundreds of adventures. Always together. Was she going to risk losing her now?

Maggie couldn't look at Jacqueline.

"I don't think Tasha's babyish," Jacqueline said. "She just has lots of energy. I really like her."

Maggie turned toward a big starfish, away from Jacqueline's gaze. In a very small voice she said,

"Well, that's what I really meant, lots of energy." She looked over at Jacqueline. "And anyway, we're all best friends together, right?"

"If you call Tasha a baby it probably means that you think you're a baby. That's what my mom says about criticizing other people." Jacqueline shrugged. "Just saying. I don't think you or Tasha are babies."

Maggie felt like a squished piece of popcorn seaweed. She was really awful to have said those things, trying so hard to be cool at Tasha's expense. "Tasha's really an awesome photographer. I mean really good. She's been taking pictures forever of Nantucket stuff, fishermen on the docks, stormy waves in winter, everything."

Jacqueline just nodded. "*Oui*, yes, she's great."

*Yelp! Whine!* A few seconds later: *Whiiiiiiine.*

Blissful! Tied up outside by their bikes. Maggie bounded to the door of the shop. A lady was leaning over Blissie.

"Oh, I'm so sorry, dear," she said to Maggie. "I was clumping my suitcase over these uneven bricks in the sidewalk, and it must have rolled right over his tail."

Maggie scooped him up in her arms. She managed a feeble, "It's okay. See, he's almost wagging it."

"What a wonderful dog," the lady said, and continued bumping her suitcase up the street.

Maggie hugged Blissie to her chest. Now she couldn't help the tears dribbling hot on her cheeks. "Good dog," she murmured in his ear. "Good little Blissie." She had been so mean about Tasha. So pathetic. "Blissie, is your tail broken?" She stroked his back, and he snuggled into her sweatshirt. "It's okay, Blissie-boy. It's okay."

"Oh no, here comes Ben on his bike," she mumbled. He waved and grinned at her from the corner. Should she pretend she didn't see him and run back inside the shop? She quickly wiped her tears off both cheeks with the back of her hand.

"Hey, Maggie." He stopped his bike. "Want to get an ice cream? Maybe we could talk about you-know-who."

Her first chance to be alone with Ben. Not fair!

"I can't, Ben," she said, hugging Blissful. "I'm picking out shells with Jacqueline. But another time, okay? I mean really, let's. Okay?" Could he tell she had just been crying?

"Sure. No problem-o."

No doubt about it. Ben looked disappointed. Even his red hair seemed darker. Ben took off down the street.

All of a sudden she was so tired she could have dropped Blissie right out of her arms. Maggie's eyes were drawn to the bench on the lawn across the street. All she wanted to do was lie down on it and go to sleep.

## CHAPTER 22

# Tasha

Maggie continued to have a sick feeling about Tasha. She had said mean things about her best friend. What kind of person would do that? She would be brave and confess it all in their journal.

The next day when Maggie, Tasha and Jacqueline settled on the driftwood log in the cove to read their journal together, Maggie was ready. Kind of. They kicked off their flip-flops. Tasha pulled a string of brown seaweed out of the sand and wove it between her toes. "Mermaid slippers!" Tasha sang out. Jacqueline and Tasha laughed. Maggie pretended to laugh.

Jacqueline grabbed another long piece of the seaweed. "I love seaweed so much." She tied hers around her ankle. "My toes are too bunched together to put seaweed in between them." Giggles from Tasha and Jacqueline.

"Here, Maggie." Tasha dangled a piece of the slimy seaweed in front of Maggie. "Decorate yourself."

*If I don't read what I wrote about Tasha in the journal right this minute, I'm never going to find the courage again,* Maggie thought. She wove the seaweed around her foot and in between her big toe and little toe.

"Picture!" Tasha said. She arranged their seaweed feet in a circle and snapped several shots.

Maggie gripped the journal in her lap. *Please, Tasha. Please talk to me after I read this. Please, please, Tasha.* Tasha huddled close on Maggie's left, and Jacqueline leaned on Maggie's shoulder on her right. Maggie took a deep breath of the salty air, her courage-builder.

Tasha hopped up to collect shells. "I'm listening," she said. She drew circles in the sand with her big toe.

"I wrote this last night," Maggie said. She started to read, and her voice came out all croaky and tight. "A few days ago I said something to Jacqueline about Tasha, my best friend since we were five. It was something mean."

"Louder, you're mumbling. Go. It's okay," Jacqueline said.

Tasha didn't appear to be listening, and that made Maggie more nervous.

She continued. "I said she was silly and couldn't sit still, like a baby. I'm so sorry I said that since it's so not true. I wish more than anything I could take it back. The dumb thing is I thought it would make me look cool and more grown-up, compared to Tasha,

143

in front of Jacqueline. I'd like to feel more grown-up sometimes. But all I feel is awful, and I know it will hurt Tasha, and I know that whenever somebody laughs at me or hurts me I feel like disappearing in the dunes so nobody can see how I believe them and feel small and ashamed inside."

Maggie read quickly. Her mouth felt drier and drier.

"So I hope so much that Tasha won't believe those dumb words I said about her. I hope she won't hate me when I read this out loud. I'm really, really sorry. Love to my Best Friend Forever (I hope), from Maggie Eva Elizabeth Cottle Greenleaf." Her heart was thumping, and she could only manage shallow breaths.

Tasha was sitting on the sand, making designs with beach stones with her back to Maggie and Jacqueline. She jumped up. Her blue eyes darkened to a deep-sea color in her round face. She shot a look at Maggie that could have knocked Maggie's head off. Tasha stalked off down the beach, arms pumping with such long, fast strides Maggie thought Tasha would split in two.

"You're right," Tasha called back. "I do hate you, Maggie. Sooo much."

Maggie didn't dare open her mouth. Finally Jacqueline said, "Do you think I should go after her?"

"Forget it."

"I think I'll go after her."

"What if Tasha never, ever, talks to me again?" Maggie heard her voice shake.

"Oh, *Dieu merci*, thank heavens, she's coming back," Jacqueline said.

Tasha plunked herself down on the log. She didn't look at Maggie. She grabbed the journal from Maggie's hands and the pen attached by a ribbon. She fixed her eyes on a clean page and started to write.

Maggie and Jacqueline sat next to her, barely moving.

When Tasha finished writing she got up, sat back down and began to read out loud.

"Here are my thoughts, by Tasha Beth Bradley Briggs. That was so, so, so mean, and it hurt me a lot. But here's the thing. Nobody has to worry that I am going to feel hurt for long because

(a) I know I am not a baby, and

(b) I know I am not silly

My father says I have a lot of imagination, like in my photographs, and even more that I am lucky to be SPONTANEOUS. Spontaneous means 'outgoing and full of good ideas.'"

Tasha's voice became clearer as she got into it. "I only hate you a little, Maggie. I never thought you would say that about me. And I'm not sure you are still my best friend. I can write this in the journal but couldn't say it out loud. The End."

Maggie touched her throat where a lump had popped up.

Jacqueline stood and hugged both Tasha and Maggie. Tasha hugged Jacqueline back and gave Maggie a quarter hug, more of a pat.

"Maybe the journal is like a fourth friend," Tasha said. "See?" She pointed to her forehead. "Imagination."

"Hey," Jacqueline said, "that took—what's the word you like, Maggie? Gumption. Both of you. To write about those things in the journal. And then read it out loud. I hope I have gumption. Sometimes I'm afraid I don't. I can't imagine I would have the nerve to write things like that."

*Jacqueline is not as sure of herself as I imagined,* Maggie thought. *She's like us. All three of us worry inside about something. Tasha runs to her mother, Jacqueline acts supercool and I run away from Cap'n Hatch and am afraid to do anything about him.*

## CHAPTER 23

# Snooping

"I'll start by saying everything is okay now, kids," Maggie's dad said at lunch the next day. "But, we had a small fire in front of the restaurant."

Maggie sucked in her breath. P. J. coughed.

"Don't worry, nobody was hurt," her mother said.

"A small fire caught on the front wooden fence around two in the morning. Luckily a policeman was patrolling the wharf and managed to put out the flames with his jacket."

"It left a filthy, burned mess," her mom said. "But Dad's replacing some of the charred parts of the fence, and it will be fine."

"Seems there was a pile of Nantucket Island newspapers by the front gate," her dad said. "Maybe a late-night walker threw a cigarette on the papers by accident. There wasn't anybody around when the policeman discovered the flames. Just a baseball cap with a boat on it, farther down the pier."

Maggie exchanged a secret look of alarm with P. J. They both knew Cap'n Hatch always wore a baseball cap with a boat on it.

"Uh, sorry about the fire, Dad. That sucks," P. J. said. "Can we help?"

"Under control, thanks."

P. J. signaled to Maggie to follow him. Outside in the backyard and away from their parents' ears, he hissed, "This is it, Maggie. We go on that boat right now, this minute. Confront Cap'n Hatch to his face about the signs and the fire outside the restaurant."

"And our evidence. His baseball cap on the pier," Maggie said. "What if he's not there?"

"We could go aboard anyway."

"Should we?"

"He may have started a fire in front of Dad's restaurant, Maffie! I think we have to."

They marched down the pier toward *Buzz Off*. That is, P. J. marched. Behind him, Maggie forced her jumpy legs to move along. Blissful walked beside her with a high, sure step, tail up in ready-to-pounce mode. No hesitation there. This gave Maggie some courage.

Wavelets that smelled like seaweed lapped against the side of the pier, and a gray fog surrounded Cap'n Hatch's boat. Maggie felt she was walking through a hovering mist of stillness and extreme quiet. Unlike her heart, which was far from still and far from quiet.

"Okay, P. J. Let's climb aboard."

Maggie swept her eyes around the deck and peered into the cabin. Nothing stirred. Not a sign of Cap'n Hatch or Scupper. She opened the cabin door and stepped down. P. J. followed.

"Let's snoop around for clues," P. J. said, flipping through papers on Cap'n Hatch's desk. "These are just weekly weather reports."

"His computer is turned off," Maggie said, "so no blinking picture of Scupper." She peeked under his old desk-chair cushion. "Look at this, P. J. A letter to Cap'n Hatch." Maggie quickly looked out through the porthole. Cap'n Hatch could loom up any second. Her eyes darted back and forth along the pier. She read the letter out loud, rushing through the words.

"From C. to H. My sweet Hatch, yes, I will meet you at 8:05 in the morning on Thursday when my ferry arrives. Behind the Chez Paul restaurant on the walkway. Your loving Carlotta."

"Cap'n Hatch has a girlfriend?" P. J. said. "And they're meeting behind Dad's restaurant Thursday morning?"

"Sounds like she likes him. Yuck," Maggie said. "I wonder if the lady knows he waves axes around at people?"

"Never mind that. They're meeting. Maybe to put up another sign against our family," P. J. said.

"We really need to catch him, P. J."

"Don't worry. We'll be right there on the walk-way behind Dad's restaurant Thursday, 8:05 a.m. sharp."

Two whole days from now. Maggie's nerves couldn't stand the wait.

## CHAPTER 24

# Surprises in the Attic

Maggie sat on the floor by her bed, brushing Blissful. Thursday was creeping up on her. What if Cap'n Hatch pounced on her and P. J. and started yelling, "Witch! Witch!"

"Stop!" Maggie said. Grammy Apple's linden tree necklace popped into her mind, all glowing and comforting. Maybe she should steel herself and go up to the back attic, creepy as it was, and find Grammy Apple's necklace in her trunk. She could wear it on Thursday for gumption.

That afternoon Maggie pulled up the latch to the back-attic door. She had to duck down to fit through the low opening. She hardly ever ventured up here.

When she had nightmares about creepy attics with giant biting spiders, *ugh*, or bats pulling her hair and trying to kiss her, *yuck*, it was always in this very back attic of her old house on Orange Street.

She climbed the steep, narrow stairs, *creeeeeek*, and walked straight into clumps of cobwebs. *Ick. Ick.* Blissful pattered close behind, undaunted by the dust.

*Click!* The door behind her closed. Dense cobwebs stretched from beams to boxes to her old rocking horse. "Where there are spiderwebs, there are spiders," she mumbled. *What about rats or mice? Or, oh, please no, dead squirrels.*

The only light came from a low square window at the far end of the attic. She was a hundred miles away from her cozy bedroom. Maggie pulled Blissful in close, in case something prickly grabbed her.

A shimmering purple trunk, Grammy Apple's for sure, stood in front of the small window. Lots of faded, round hatboxes, piled one on top of the other and tied with wide, pale ribbons, nestled on either side of the trunk.

A soft hush suddenly stirred inside Maggie. Her nervous feelings began to tiptoe bit by bit back down the attic stairs, replaced by a sense of dreaminess. Something wonderful was about to happen. She could feel it.

Maggie glanced at a clean little rug in front of the trunk and felt it was inviting her to sit down. She got comfortable and crossed her legs. Blissful went for the rug, too, and settled on his side, his head curving around to his feet, completely relaxed. Maggie laughed. Did he imagine he was a round doughnut?

*Click*

The trunk lock opened by itself. Maggie pushed up the heavy top and breathed in the strong, delicious wafts of honey and lemon peel.

"You're telling me it's okay to look in your trunk. Right, Grammy Apple?" Another big swoosh of honey and lemon peel circled softly around her and answered her question.

The first thing Maggie saw was a scruffy leopard-skin fur coat. It took up a lot of space. She dug down farther, and her fingers touched Grammy Apple's necklace. Of course Grammy Apple wanted her to wear it on Thursday for gumption when she confronted Cap'n Hatch. She put it around her neck and touched the linden tree charm. The necklace felt just right, all golden and gleaming.

Now for the round hatboxes piled willy-nilly around the purple trunk. Grammy Apple sure must have loved wearing hats. Maggie guessed she decorated the hatboxes herself with delicate flowered wallpaper. She looked more closely at the covers. This could be faded handwriting. Recipes! Here's one for Apple Pan Dowdy, another for Rhubarb and Ginger Jam and one for Half-Moon Cookies.

Everything her mother made. So her Grammy Apple had been a baker, and her mom was a baker, and Maggie loved to bake these very same recipes with her mom. Maggie closed her eyes and imagined herself, Mom and Grammy Apple in the kitchen baking together, cozy and warm. She could even smell wafts of gingerbread puffing up in the oven, filling the kitchen with deliciousness.

One of the faded hatbox ribbons untied itself, and the cover fell off. Blissful lifted his head and wagged his tail like crazy. "I know, Blissie. There's more!" An old hat, a red felt thing with a wrinkled pink silk rose, rustled in the tissue. Maggie plopped it on her head. Hadn't she just drawn herself in this very hat in the three-way journal? She smiled at Blissful. "Now that's witchy, Blissie."

Maggie rustled around in the rest of the tissue and found an envelope with her name on it:

*To my adored grandaughter*
*Maggie Eva Elizabeth Cottle Greenleaf*
*When she is ready to share magic with me*

*Wow.* The honey and lemon peel scent was just as fresh as if the linden tree were growing right out of the sagging attic floorboards. Maggie breathed it in, straight down to her heart.

A tiny silver mirror slipped out of the red envelope onto her lap. There was also a letter inside.

When you are unsure of your
beautiful heart and spirit,
Just look in this hand mirror
Where you can always see
What wonder beams inside you.
I love who you are every minute
Of your day and night.
Grammy Apple

Maggie put the silver hand mirror in her pocket, closed her eyes and flattened Grammy Apple's letter against her chest. She rested her head on the trunk. She stayed that way for a long quiet time. She didn't want to leave.

CHAPTER 25

# Thursday Arrives

Maggie paced back and forth in her room. It was almost 7:35 in the morning, and P. J. wasn't even dressed. She had hardly eaten all day yesterday. Last night she woke up three times, turning in rumpled sheets from one side to the other, touching the linden tree necklace on her neck.

At exactly 8:05, Maggie and P. J. hid themselves behind a barrel on the walkway in back of the restaurant. There wasn't a person in sight, only Maggie's seagull friends flapping their wings high over the shoreline.

"Uh-oh. Here comes somebody," Maggie said in a very quiet voice. She pulled P. J. closer in behind the barrel.

A short, plump lady rounded the corner of the walkway. She had gray curls and carried a red canvas tote bag. Maggie thought she had a kind face, the sort of person who carried candy treats in her pocket.

"That's her! She has a *C* on her bag," P. J. whispered. "For Carlotta."

"And it's big enough to hold a sign," Maggie added.

"I've seen that lady before," P. J. said. "When Ben and I were peeking through the window of The Tipsy Rose pub looking to catch Cap'n Hatch doing something suspicious. That same lady was petting Scupper and watching Cap'n Hatch play pool."

Maggie nudged P. J. in the ribs. "Shh. There he is, coming down the walkway."

Without even a "hello," Cap'n Hatch wrapped the lady up in his arms. Holding on to the windowsill, he slowly went down on one knee. He rummaged in his jacket pocket and pulled out a small box.

The lady gasped and put her hand on her mouth.

"What the heck is he doing?" P. J. whispered.

"He doesn't look like he can get back up," Maggie said, keeping her voice low, low, low.

Cap'n Hatch fumbled with the lid of the box and took out a sparkly ring. "Carlotta, please marry me!"

"Get up off your knees, you silly man. Of course I'll marry you." She helped him up.

He slipped the sparkly ring on her finger.

P. J. shook his head. "Doesn't look like he's thinking much about putting up signs."

"Why would that lady ever want to marry *him*? He's such an old grump," Maggie said. *Darn.* She just couldn't seem to catch Cap'n Hatch doing anything wrong. He'd probably terrorize her forever— her whole life, with his zip-your-mouth signs.

Maggie and P. J. slipped away unnoticed by the lovebirds.

"Oh boy. Now what, P. J.?" Maggie said.

CHAPTER 26

# The Most Lovely Wonderful Thing Happened

The next day Maggie slipped her skirt over her bathing suit and focused her thoughts on oyster-catchers with long red bills. She had just the right reds in her pastel box to capture that very color, depending on the light, of course. If the oyster-catcher drawing came out eye-catching, she would put it right in front of her tent at the art fair. Red always attracted attention, and she wanted to make sure customers moseyed over in her direction, bedazzled by her bright colors.

Jacqueline and her mother, Madame Bonnard, would be here any minute for a drive out to Great Point, the tippy end of Nantucket. It was just the distraction Maggie needed, since spying on Cap'n Hatch behind her father's restaurant had turned out to be a fizzle. Madame Bonnard was bringing a *pique-nique*—the funny French word for picnic, hopefully with chocolate croissants.

Tasha couldn't come. She was in photography class.

Maggie zipped her skirt, slipped a rubber band around her box of pastels and nestled them into her beach bag. Sketch pad, beach towel, what else? She plopped Grammy Apple's old red hat with the pink rose on her head.

*Shuffle, shuffle.*

Maggie whirled around. There was something hazy . . . a person . . . sitting on top of her dressing table . . . fluffy white hair, a long shawl with silver dots around her shoulders . . . and the linden tree necklace shining on her neck.

A faraway voice drifted into Maggie's ears. It sounded like,

*My darling girl . . .*

"Grammy Apple," Maggie whispered. She stared and stared.

Grammy Apple opened her arms wide, as if to cuddle Maggie inside a big hug. *Whoosh!* A strong waft of honey and lemon peel floated around them.

Maggie took a careful step closer. "Is this really happening, Grammy Apple?" Maggie felt light, practically airborne, and full of her Grammy's love.

*Take my letter from the hatbox with you today. It will help you find your gumption with your father. You can do it. Look in the hand mirror I gave you too. For reassurance . . .*

She blew Maggie a kiss full of stars and then—oh! She vanished.

Maggie fixed her gaze on her dressing table without moving an eyelash, practically not breathing. Was she dreaming?

Jacqueline! She would be bouncing up the stairs any second. Maggie quickly took Grammy Apple's letter from her bedside table drawer and stuffed it in her skirt pocket. She held up the hand mirror. There she was, full of gumption, just like Grammy Apple promised. She put the mirror back in the drawer.

"Hey, Maggie," Jacqueline called from downstairs. "Ready?"

She heard Jacqueline's wooden-soled sandals clomping up the stairs. She had four seconds to act as if nothing had happened. But not before she let the whispers and fragrance of Grammy Apple wash through her again.

*I really, really saw her. Sitting right there, smiling at me all lovey.* Maggie hugged herself and closed her eyes.

*I think Grammy Apple believes I have gumption already. She said her letter and the mirror would help me find it. She didn't say the letter would do it for me.*

"Hi," Jacqueline huffed. "I ran. My mom is coming in a few minutes."

"Hey, Jacqueline," Maggie said, keeping her voice as calm as possible. "That's a really pretty skirt."

"I like yours. I love the jellyfish on it. Let's switch!" Jacqueline started slipping her skirt over her head. She had on a bright yellow bathing suit.

Maggie hesitated. What about Grammy Apple's letter in her pocket?

"It'll be fun," Jacqueline persisted.

They pulled their skirts over their heads. Maggie managed to slip the letter out of her pocket and into the deep pocket in Jacqueline's skirt. Jacqueline didn't notice.

"That looks really pretty on you, Maggie." Jacqueline wiggled into Maggie's skirt.

"Thanks. And mine looks great on you. Keep it, Jacqueline. It has jellyfish to remind you of Nantucket when you're back in Paris."

Maggie checked herself out in the long mirror on the back of her door. The short skirt had fancy ruffles and yes, Maggie liked the way it swirled around her legs. She put her hand down into the deep pocket to reassure herself that the letter was still there.

"*Allons-y*. Let's go," Jacqueline said as they ran down the stairs. "My mom and I have never been out to Great Point. We can beachcomb for special shells and stuff. Like seaweed. Maybe with a little seahorse tangled inside."

"Finding a seahorse is extremely doubtful," Maggie said. Only part of her was here with Jacqueline. Seeing her Grammy Apple was a longing that had come true. Grammy Apple had *talked* to her.

"I know I'm going to find the best seaweed out there on Great Point," Jacqueline said.

Nobody on all of Nantucket was as crazy about seaweed as Jacqueline. She had a collection of sea lettuce, Irish moss and various kinds of kelp. She planned to take the whole smelly stash back with her to Paris at the end of the summer. Maggie had never known anyone so obsessed. But since Jacqueline lived in a big city with no seaweed, Maggie understood.

In the kitchen Maggie's parents were getting ready to go to the restaurant.

"Where did you get that pretty skirt, Maggie?" her mother asked.

"Jacqueline and I exchanged skirts for the beach picnic. It's from Paris." Maggie swept the ruffled skirt wide and twirled.

"Well, it shows off your legs, Toothpick," her father said with a chuckle.

Maggie forced her brave humiliation smile. *Here we go again. Forget about his promise not to tease me,* she told herself. *I wonder if Maggie One's father ever said such a thing to her? Like kidding her about chubby legs or something? What about Grammy Apple's letter? Wasn't it supposed to help me?* Maggie dropped her head down, her face burning hot. She couldn't talk. Sticking her finger in her ear, the sign for her father to stop teasing, was ridiculous, and she wouldn't do it.

To make matters much worse, her father started to talk with a crazy French accent. "Zees eez too many of zee ruffles, no? See I speak very good zee

French." He looked at Jacqueline. "Just kidding around. You don't sound like that."

Jacqueline didn't react to Maggie's father. She just looked at him. Then, in a respectful tone she said, "Oh, I like my accent. I'm proud to be French."

On the way outside Jacqueline said, "I don't think you have toothpick legs at all. They're so nice and long. Be happy you don't have fat ankles like me. You look like a ballerina."

Maggie's skirt rustled. She felt in her pocket for the hatbox letter. Her fingers tingled when she touched it, and something deep inside her went *ker-klunk*. Suddenly, the whole scene with her father in the kitchen began to lose its sting.

*Beep! Beep!* "There's your mom in the Jeep, Jacqueline. Wait one minute, okay? I'll be right back." Maggie dashed back to the kitchen.

"Hey, Dad," she said. She put her hand in her pocket and held on to Grammy Apple's letter. "I want to tell you I know you're just kidding about calling me 'toothpick legs' and trying to talk like Jacqueline. You just like people to laugh at your jokes no matter how it makes them feel. I hate when you call me 'toothpick legs.' You said you wouldn't."

There. She said it. She kept her eyes on her father and her hand on the letter.

Her dad walked over and hugged her. "Aw, I'm really sorry, Maggie-girl. Bad habit. Of course I'm just kidding." He put his hand over his heart. "No more 'toothpick legs,' I promise."

He gave her another hug. It felt like he meant it. At least he took the blame this time. She didn't think he caught the part about how his jokes could hurt people.

Maggie walked out of the kitchen with a bounce. *Why haven't I ever stood up to Daddy before?*

*Because, Maggie darling, it was reeeeeally hard . . .*

Grammy Apple again. She took a big, lovely breath of the honey and lemon peel scent wafting around her. Sticking up for herself sure felt good. And her dad didn't even seem angry. He seemed happy.

Maggie put her hand back in her pocket. No letter. It had done its work, and she knew it was back upstairs in her bedside table drawer. Right next to Grammy's linden tree necklace and the hand mirror.

## CHAPTER 27

# Great Point

"I lowered the air in the tires so we won't get stuck in the sand," Madame Bonnard said. "Thanks for the tip, Maggie. This will be some adventure, girls! I put the top down too." She swerved the red Jeep onto the beach and out toward Great Point. Maggie and Jacqueline laughed and held on.

A huge black raven with a startling wingspread swooped down to the windshield of the open Jeep. Maggie scrunched her eyes closed and cringed. The raven hovered and stared inside, right at Jacqueline, looking like he might attack. *Oh no.* Maggie clenched her hands.

A direct glare from a black raven meant something bad was going to happen to that person. It was probably just a dumb old Nantucket story—except that the raven was peering right into Jacqueline's face.

"Oooo, help!" Jacqueline said. "He's right here!" She flapped her arms at him. Her mom tried to speed up the car. "Shoo, shoo!" she called out at him. The raven opened his beak. *Caw, caaaaaw!*

The raven swooped off, his squawks disappearing over the ocean.

"It's nothing," Maggie said, trying to calm the others. "He just came a little close." But she had never seen such a big raven so near before.

"Whew," Madame Bonnard said. "Not the friendliest bird I've ever seen."

The red Jeep bumped and bounced along midway between the dunes and the breaking waves. "Oops," she called out as she tried hard to stay in the tracks left by other Jeeps and trucks. Strong sea breezes whooshed through their hair and helped to whisk away the creepy feeling left behind by the raven and his glassy ink-black eyes.

"Doesn't that salty breeze smell wonderful?" Madame Bonnard took a long sniff with her face to the sky. She sang a pretty French song as they jounced along the beach. She stopped singing for a moment and glanced through the rearview mirror at Maggie in the back seat. "I heard about the signs outside your father's restaurant. I'm sorry. But how odd they're about witches." She cleared her throat and gave Maggie a strange look.

Maggie squished down a little lower in her seat and said nothing. *Madame Bonnard hates witches. That's obvious. Maybe she put up the signs.* Maggie shook the thought out of her head. *Don't be crazy, Maggie. Of course she didn't put up the signs.*

Jacqueline said nothing. Maggie still wasn't sure how Jacqueline really felt about witches. *Did Jacqueline put up the signs? Stop it, Maggie. Don't be ridiculous. Of course it's Cap'n Hatch. He's the one giving me the nasty zip-your-mouth signs.*

They began to cruise, chugging along a smoother part of the beach out toward the tip of the island. Maggie searched for a glimpse of an oystercatcher and his red bill. None to be seen. Oh well, you had to be lucky. All she saw were a few fat gray-and-white seagulls hanging around an old deserted shack by the dunes.

"It's getting really windy, girls," Madame Bonnard said.

Maggie noticed the wind whipping up the surf. The lighthouse at the tip of the island grew closer and closer.

"Oh, look, you can see water on both sides," Jacqueline said. She popped out of her seat and waved her arms around. *Bump. Oops.* Her mother reached over and yanked her back down.

"Jacqueline! A little sense, please," her mother said. "Seat belt back on, *tout de suite*, right now. You must control this habit of yours—giving in to the first impulse that jumps into your head!"

They chose a spot near the lighthouse to park the car. There were only a couple of fishermen in high rubber boots out there surf casting.

"What are you fishing for?" Jacqueline's mother called out to them.

"Blues and striped bass," one yelled back. "It's beginning to surf up pretty good out here. Don't think about swimming." He waved.

The girls pulled off their skirts and sweatshirts and took off to beachcomb. The sun was nice and hot despite the breezes. They left Jacqueline's mother settling into her beach chair.

"Be careful," she called after them, lifting up the front of her purple straw hat. "Just go as far as that old shack we passed and then come back for the *pique-nique*, okay? Bring me back a starfish."

They laughed and ran on up the beach, gusty breezes pricking their legs with sand.

"Want to know the latest from Henri and Corby, my brother-brats?" Jacqueline said. "This morning they piled all my shoes way in the back of the kitchen cabinet while my mom was up in the attic looking for the beach umbrella. The twins are beyond irritating. They wouldn't stop hooting and laughing. I couldn't imagine where all my shoes had gone! And my boots."

"Really? It's hard for me to picture Corby being so full of mischief. He really concentrates when he's with me in drawing class," Maggie said.

"Maybe in that situation he's quiet. But the two of them together? They cook up catastrophes. Totally irritating ones."

Maggie and Jacqueline meandered up the beach by the dunes, not talking much, happy to scour around for a hidden starfish or periwinkle shells. An extra sharp wind skimmed across the sand. Maggie looked at the waves and saw them whip up high to a furious froth. She frowned.

Jacqueline wandered down to the shoreline. She was heading closer to the water, and Maggie hurried to catch up with her. A big clump of bright lime-green sea lettuce tossed in the churning waves, and Jacqueline darted right toward it.

## CHAPTER 18

# The Irresistible Sea Lettuce

*S*he wouldn't! Maggie gulped. "Hey! No! Jacqueline! Don't you dare go near those waves!" Maggie bolted after her.

"It's lettuce! For my seaweed collection. C'mon, Maggie," she yelled over the roar of the crashing surf. "It's not so far out." Jacqueline was now up to her waist in the churning water. "I'll grab it and come right back out."

Maggie sprang after Jacqueline. "No way!" she hollered. "Stop!" She knew Jacqueline could only dog paddle. And not very well. "Jacqueline! Come out!" She screamed louder. "You heard the fishermen. No going in the water!"

Maggie flew down to the high, angry waves, her heart thumping with fright. The beach was so empty. No lifeguards. They were totally alone.

"Jacqueline!" she screamed. "Stop! Stop! Don't go in any deeper! Come OUT!" Maggie had been swimming since she was three years old. She was a superstrong swimmer. She wouldn't dream of going into the water with waves like this.

"There it is!" Jacqueline dashed farther out in the surf to snatch the sea lettuce. It was just within her reach. Before Maggie could blink Jacqueline was sucked down into the center of a high, dark, crashing wave. She disappeared.

A bolt of terror shot through Maggie's body.

Plunge.

She dove in. The freezing current pulled her away from shore.

"JACQUELINE!"

A wave roared over Maggie's head. It smacked her in the face with a salty force. Her eyes stung, and she blinked hard. She fought with all her strength to stay in control. *Oh my God. Jacqueline!*

### CRASH! BOOM!

"Jacqueline!"

The sucking current yanked at Maggie's body.

In a blink it pulled her rapidly out to sea.

Her arms and legs were useless, and she was over her head in a roiling mass of angry waves.

A riptide! They were caught in a riptide!

Terror strangled her. She went completely stiff, like a clump of driftwood about to be pulled into the ocean depths. A wild panic blackened her vision.

### SMACK!

A wave hit her head, and she felt her breath returning and her heart hammering. A reserve of super-strength and fight raced through her arms, legs and insides.

She willed every muscle to help her swivel toward shore and over to Jacqueline. These waves were giant arms yanking her out to sea.

"Jacqueline! I'm here!" she yelled. A rush of seawater filled her mouth. She gagged and spit it out. "I'm here!"

Jacqueline's drenched head and open mouth surfaced a good distance away. Maggie heard a faint, "I can't. *Maman!*" Jacqueline was sinking. Maggie powered her way toward her.

Jacqueline—rising, sinking,

gasping out salty water,

her yellow bathing suit appearing and disappearing in the wild surf.

*CRASH BOOM!*

*CRASH BOOM!*

Then, the undertow gave them a fraction of a second's grace, and a wave bumped Maggie up against Jacqueline. Maggie grabbed her like a muscular water snake that wasn't about to loosen its grip.

They were so far away from the shore. Maggie's heart clenched. She tried to not pay attention to a rotten fishy smell around her.

**WHOOSH**

*You can do this, Maggie. You can. You can. Believe it and you will saaaave your friend . . .*

But Maggie barely noticed Grammy Apple's voice floating above the roaring surf.

"The shoreline. Where is the shoreline?" Maggie gasped out loud. The sound of her own voice released her courage. With all the strength she had ever pulled out of herself, Maggie forced her strokes to go parallel to the beach. She held Jacqueline against her so hard she felt her friend's bones.

Jacqueline thrashed her arms about, hitting Maggie. Maggie knew it was involuntary panic. "Go limp, Jacqueline! Don't fight! I've got you." Another wave engulfed them in a mighty pull farther out to sea.

She could get them out of this riptide. She could. Just get parallel to the shore. Stay parallel. Swim steady. Keep swimming. Steady. Stay parallel. Parallel.

"It's okay, Jacqueline. I'VE GOT YOU."

Focus, focus. Parallel. There! The lighthouse, way down the beach. Maggie's head hurt—like a rock inside her head, hitting her behind the eyes. She heard nothing. No gulls calling, no crashing surf.

Jacqueline gagged on saltwater. Maggie tightened her water-snake hold around Jacqueline's slippery shoulders. "I've got you. I've got you. Keep your mouth closed." Maggie's exhausted muscles were screaming silently, her wrist, elbow and whole arm were one dull pain from the strain.

Suddenly, in a lucky split-second moment, Maggie wrenched them both free of the terrifying current that had gripped their bodies like the sucking tentacles of a giant octopus. She swam them into shore with a push from a breaking wave and dragged Jacqueline out of the water onto the sand. Maggie, beyond exhausted, didn't let go of Jacqueline.

Jacqueline sobbed out little squawks, like a terrified baby seagull. Maggie couldn't calm her own shaking legs and knees and shoulders. They were both on their knees clinging to each other.

## CHAPTER 29

# A Changed Maggie

Three older boys were having a catch just up the beach. Maggie stood up halfway, keeping one hand on Jacqueline. She shouted, "Hey! Help us! Over here! Help. Over here."

The boys ran down the beach toward them, waving and calling out, "We're coming!"

Maggie panted, "We got caught in the rip." She sunk back on her knees, still holding on to Jacqueline.

"Whoa. Not good," one of the boys said. They gave the girls their beach towels. Jacqueline sobbed and shook all over.

"Do you have your phone?" Maggie asked the boys. "Can you please call my friend's mother?"

"There's no service on the beach, maybe in the dunes," one of the boys said.

Maggie slapped herself on the forehead. "Of course, I know that. Her mom's on the beach, no service there either." She pointed toward the lighthouse.

"We have a car," said the older boy. He ran toward the dunes. "I'll bring her back. What does she look like?"

"Big purple hat, sitting under a beach umbrella. She was the only one out at the Point except for two fishermen." Maggie's breath was still coming out in short little puffs.

The boy leaped up the dunes to his car. "Five minutes," he yelled down. He held up his hand and spread his five fingers wide. "Don't worry. I'll be right back with her mother."

"He's a fast driver," one of the boys said. "He'll speed."

Maggie put her arms around Jacqueline, who was shaking more than before.

"We did it. We're safe. Your mom's coming." Maggie rubbed Jacqueline's arms and hands, still blue and ice-cold. Her own insides were a violent, tumbling surf, and she was shaking too. "We're safe. We're safe."

The younger boy tried to slip a pink-and-white slipper shell into Jacqueline's hands. "Here, take this."

The shell fell through Jacqueline's fingers unnoticed. Her eyes were rolling. Maggie gently spoke in her ear, "You're okay now. Your mom's coming. We're safe." These words soothed Maggie too. In the middle of that riptide, when every ounce of her fought the overpowering pull out to sea, she wasn't fully conscious of how terrified she had been. Only now, with her knees, legs and feet planted safely in the sand, did the whole horror wash over her. Maggie clutched Jacqueline as hard as Jacqueline was clutching her.

The waves crashed on, a fury of foam.

*BOOM shhhhhhhh*

*BOOM shhhhhhhhhh*

*BOOM shhhhhhhhhhhh*

The older boy arrived with Jacqueline's mother, whose eyes were wild with panic. She dashed down the dunes and sunk to her knees. *"C'est bien.* It's okay now." She enfolded both girls in her arms, rubbing their backs.

"Maggie saved me," Jacqueline sobbed. "I . . . can't . . . stop," she gulped into her mother's chest. A second later she threw up on the sand. Her mother held her hair back and wiped Jacqueline's mouth with the beach towel.

She smoothed Jacqueline's forehead. "It's all right now, darling. You are both very brave. You're my brave Jacqueline, right, my angel?" She didn't let go of her daughter, and at the same time she held Maggie closer. *"Merci, merci,* sweet, strong Maggie." She covered Maggie's face with grateful kisses filled with tears.

Maggie's shaking began to slow down. Wrapped in the beach towel, she held on to Madame Bonnard and let her body relax a bit with relief. Why wasn't she crying like Jacqueline?

"This wonderful young man has offered to drive us all back in the Jeep," Madame Bonnard said. "Maggie, *chérie*, we'll drop you off at your parents' restaurant."

The other two boys kept a respectful distance.

"Glad everything is okay," one said.

"Yeah, wow, you guys were lucky," the younger one added. "Don't worry about the beach towels. Keep them." The boys jogged down the beach to pick up their car.

Maggie climbed in the back seat of the Jeep and closed her eyes, which were finally filling with tears. She pulled the beach towel high around her shoulders, wrapped her arms around herself and breathed slowly. Finding her strength in the midst of terror was extraordinary. She'd been choked with terror, more than she'd ever been in her life. But . . . yes . . . in the middle of those angry waves she had tapped a bottomless well of courage that lived deep inside her. What she had just done was beyond brave, and Maggie knew it, way down. She, Maggie Greenleaf, had the heart to take on a powerful riptide that could so easily have washed them both out to sea.

*Whoosh* . . . She inhaled a waft of honey and lemon peel. It smelled so sweet and nice.

*And you did it yourself, my brave granddaughter . . .*

Yes, Grammy Apple, I did it myself.

"Toothpick legs" had saved a life.

## CHAPTER 30

# Comfort

Jacqueline's mom brought Maggie to the restaurant and her parents. Maggie and her mom held each other so tightly, both sobbing with relief.

"Maggie, oh, Maggie." Her mother could barely talk.

"Thank God, thank God," her dad said. "Here, put this on." He bundled Maggie in his sweatshirt, which fell to her knees. They both put their arms around Maggie and held her there for a long time. She had short fits of shivers, and her mom pulled the hood around Maggie's head.

Normally her father's face was suntanned. Now it was as white as chalk. "Thank God," he managed to say again through tears. "I'm so proud of you, my incredibly brave girl." He dragged the big armchair from his office into a corner of the restaurant kitchen. Maggie snuggled into the soft cushions and watched the cooks scurry and chop and sauté. At first the smell of potatoes roasting and onions sautéing in fragrant herbs made her queasy. But as she settled in and stopped shivering, the cooking smells became soothing and familiar. Her mom had wanted to take her right home to rest, but Maggie just felt like sinking into the soft chair and being around the restaurant bustle for a while.

Maggie stared at her arms that had fought the sucking current so hard. They were the same arms she had yesterday. But they were different now. Stronger. Not like picking-up-stuff stronger. Courage-stronger.

About an hour later her mother took off her apron and stroked Maggie's head, her arms, tears flowing again. "Let's go home now, Maggie."

Her mother pulled the comforter up to Maggie's chin and tucked it around her shoulders. Maggie sunk into her parents' bed, a baby gull snuggled in its nest. Blissful settled himself right against her. He put his paw on her head, and she was sure he gave her an admiring look, as if he were proud of her too. She fell fast asleep.

Several hours later Maggie woke up and smelled macaroni and cheese. Her mom tiptoed in and sat down close to her. "How do you feel, darling? Ready for a little snack?" Her mother caressed her cheek.

Maggie turned over and managed a weak smile. "Yes, please." She looked into her mom's eyes. "When I was grabbing for Jacqueline in the waves, I smelled the honey and lemon peel, and I heard Grammy Apple say I could do it. Then I kept swimming stronger and stronger without Grammy Apple's smell or words. By myself."

Her mother hugged her and held Maggie's hand, like she never, ever, wanted to let go of her.

"I spoke to Madame Bonnard. Jacqueline slept a long time too. And she's okay."

Maggie filled up with tears. She and Jacqueline were bound together now in a horrifying experience that was theirs alone.

In the kitchen, just as Maggie was finishing the last bite of her mac and cheese, she heard a knock on the door.

"Hello there, Corby," her mother said. "Come in."

"My mother sent this over for Maggie, for saving my sister and stuff. Here." Corby handed Maggie a small silver box with pearls on top. "It's from Paris, where we live."

"It's so beautiful. That's so nice. Thank you. Where's Henri?" Maggie asked.

"Um, well, he was afraid to come. On account of that you are witches."

Her mother's eyebrows shot up. Maggie gulped and dropped her fork.

"I told Maggie *I* wasn't afraid of witches because if Maggie is one, then witches are really nice," he said.

Maggie's mom started to say something, then stopped and stepped back. Maggie saw that her mother wanted her to handle this.

"What do you think a witch is, Corby?" Maggie asked in a gentle voice.

"I don't know. Pretend? Maybe someone who puts children in big pots and cooks them for dinner?" Corby looked like he thought the cooking children idea might be true.

"Nothing like that, Corby," Maggie said.

"Well, what's it like then?" he asked.

"I can only speak for myself, but my Grammy Apple was a magical person; some people called her a witch, and I'm a magical person too—sometimes. I can hear my Grammy Apple telling me to draw, draw, draw. And I can see magical things to sketch like seagulls doing cartwheels. And tons of other stuff."

Corby's eyes got wide. "That doesn't sound so wicked."

"It's not," said Maggie. "It's wonderful."

He ran out. "People shouldn't be mean to you because you're a witch," he called back over his shoulder. "You can't help it." He turned and added, "I'm going to talk to Henri about witches. Straighten him out. Maybe when he knows the truth he won't be scared."

# CHAPTER 31

# Magic in the Attic

The next day in her bedroom Maggie found a note on her pillow. It smelled of honey and lemon peel. She read it out loud.

Have a ritual by my trunk in the back attic with Tasha and Jacqueline. It may lead you to something you should know about the signs.

Before you begin, say out loud, "So Mote It Be." That means "May It Happen" in magic talk.

Maggie paused. "I love that phrase, 'So Mote It Be.' So witchy!" She continued.

Here's what you will need.
- A silver pitcher
- A big bowl
- A small bag of clean beach sand
- Some salt

Now here's what you do.

Maggie memorized Grammy Apple's instructions, and the note disappeared.

On a blue-sky-yellow-sun afternoon, nothing stirred around the old boat beached on the sand in the harbor where Maggie's art class met in the mornings. The brown cattails in the grasses by the boat looked like hot dogs on long sticks, and they didn't move. Soft baby waves barely plopped on the shore. The old boat was a cozy place to make plans for their magic ritual. Maggie lifted the brim of her red hat with the pink rose and waved to Tasha and Jacqueline. They were leaning their bikes against a big rock and ran to meet her in the boat.

"I'll help any way I can, Maggie," Jacqueline said.

"Me too," Tasha said.

Maggie hoped so much that she and Tasha were really best friends again, after the journal and all. Tasha was looking at Maggie in her regular cheerful way, thank goodness. If her own heart were half the size of Tasha's she would be lucky. Tasha knew how to forgive people. *I wonder if I'm like that. I don't think I could ever forgive Cap'n Hatch.*

The smallest doubt niggled into Maggie's mind. *What if Cap'n Hatch wasn't the one putting up the signs? No, not possible. There's no one else. Right?*

Tasha and Jacqueline climbed into the boat.

"I just want you both to know," Jacqueline said, "that since Maggie saved me in the riptide? I feel different. Inside, I mean." She spread her arms wide. "I feel bigger. Like miracles can happen." She grinned at Maggie and Tasha. "Like acrobatic seagulls and dune grasses that go . . ." She stood up and did a complete backbend in the boat.

Maggie and Tasha clapped.

"But yikes," Tasha said. "That riptide. Seriously scary. I'm so glad you're both okay." Tasha shook her head. Her blue eyes got wide. "Maggie, you were really, really strong and brave."

Maggie knew she was strong and brave, but it sure felt good to hear Tasha say it.

"I will never stop remembering how you pulled me out of that ocean, Maggie," Jacqueline said with tears in her eyes.

Maggie smiled at her. How stupid to have thought only Jacqueline was cool. They were all cool—Tasha, Jacqueline and herself. Each in their own way. Maggie looked at Tasha's concerned face. Tasha had been truly horrified at the idea of anything happening to Maggie in the riptide. If anything, Maggie thought, Tasha was the most grown-up of all three of them. She was able to get beyond Maggie's mean words about her and forgive her. There was nothing babyish about forgiving. Maggie gave Tasha a "thank goodness we're still best friends" look and said, "Thanks for absolutely everything, Tasha."

Maggie took a deep breath, filled with the closeness she felt for her two friends, each in a different way.

"So let's finalize our plans for our magic ritual," she said, adjusting Grammy Apple's red hat with the pink rose. Without saying anything about Cap'n Hatch she added, "Let's hope we get some hint about who is putting up the signs."

She closed her eyes and begged silently, *Please, please, Grammy Apple. Just show us something, like a picture of his baseball cap or Scupper. The meeting behind the restaurant was such a flop. I can tell you scold him through his apple tattoo when it itches and burns. I really need your help.*

"Okay," Maggie said, coming back to the ritual plans. "We just go up to my back attic, sit in a circle in front of Grammy Apple's trunk, stare down into a bowl of ocean water, wish real hard for clues about the signs and see if anything appears. That's what Grammy Apple said in her note." She took a pad and pencil out of her backpack.

"I have a question," Jacqueline said. "I've never seen magic before. Will it hurt?"

"I hope not," Tasha said. "My mom believes in it and says if we use magic to help someone we're fine. Right, Maggie? Don't you think Grammy Apple would say that?"

A big waft of honey and lemon peel swirled around them.

"There's our answer," Maggie said. "Let's just be nervous, really nervous even, and go ahead anyway, right?"

"So we need a small bag of sand to put in the bowl," Maggie said. "Tasha can bring that."

"What can I bring?" Jacqueline said.

"A small pitcher of saltwater," Maggie said. "Are you okay with that? Tasha and I will wade in with you. Look, it's totally calm here in the harbor. Little baby ripples, no big ocean waves."

Maggie gave this chore to Jacqueline on purpose. Hopefully it would get her back in the water and she wouldn't be so afraid of it. Maggie ruffled around in her backpack and pulled out a silver pitcher. "Here, for the water and our first spell."

"Spell?" Jacqueline said.

"You cast a spell, like sitting quietly and clearing out your mind so answers about the signs can come in."

Jacqueline clutched the pitcher and headed to the water. Maggie and Tasha were right there at her side. Jacqueline stopped.

"I'm good. I can do it. Go back to the boat." She walked away from them.

Jacqueline waded into the harbor and picked her way carefully past the thin saltwater grasses that brushed against her legs, out to the little wavelets that reached her knees. She scooped up the water into the pitcher, turned to her friends and held the pitcher up high over her head. Her huge smile could have perked up sleepy horseshoe crabs and caused the seagulls to flap their wings and clap.

Maggie handed Tasha a plastic bag and a big wooden spoon. Tasha made her way through the tall joe-pye weed and sea lavender that grew on the beach. She dug a few spoonfuls of undisturbed sand, where nobody had trampled on it, per Grammy Apple's instructions. She poured it into the plastic bag. Maggie saw that Tasha couldn't stop herself from taking her camera out of her pocket and snapping a few pictures of the tight pink buds on the joe-pye weed. Maggie smiled. Someday Tasha might make photography books about Nantucket or have exhibits and become famous. *Thank goodness things are okay between us.*

"Be at my house this afternoon at three, okay?" Maggie said to Jacqueline and Tasha. "Let's wear nice clothes, something kind of soft and respectful."

"Respectful of Grammy Apple?" Tasha asked.

"Sort of. Respectful of the magic I hope we can make happen."

## CHAPTER 32

# Deep Down in the Lavender Bowl

Just before the girls were to arrive at Maggie's house, her mother pulled Maggie aside. "I'm going to let you use this lavender bowl for your first ritual. It's milky moon crystal and belonged to your Grammy Apple."

Maggie touched the angels sculpted around the rim.

"For good Grammy Apple magic," her mother added. The amber glints in her mother's eyes deepened into a darker brown than usual. "Grammy

Apple's magic is not trick magic, Maggie, like pulling rabbits out of hats. She tried to tell me many times that real and true magic means you can see something or feel something beyond what you usually see or feel." She touched Maggie's cheek. "But you have to really want to. And sometimes it doesn't work."

"I love when you talk about Grammy Apple, Mommy. Thanks for letting us use her bowl."

"It's making your Grammy Apple happy, that's

 for sure. And I'm beginning to understand your Grammy and me a little better now. I can even remember funny things about her. Not just embarrassing things." She handed Maggie the bowl. It was quite heavy, like something that belonged in a museum.

"Like what funny things?"

"Well, for one thing, Grammy Apple almost named me Lettuce! I would have ended up Lettuce Greenleaf, wife of a chef." They burst out laughing. She put her hands on Maggie's shoulders. "I hope you have a beautiful ritual, darling."

Maggie looked into her mother's brown eyes with their amber glints and saw her mother happy.

Tasha and Jacqueline arrived with the sand and the sloshy seawater. Tasha had brushed out her braids and put a silk ribbon in her long hair. "For respect for Grammy Apple," she said.

Jacqueline had put on a soft dress the color of lemons and honey. "For respect for Grammy Apple's magic."

And Maggie had changed into her prettiest white lacy top. She pinned a small bunch of pale-yellow linden tree flowers on her collar. In Grammy Apple's honor. "For respect for the magic in all three of us."

They climbed up the steep staircase to the back attic. Tasha clutched the bag of sand, Jacqueline balanced the pitcher of seawater and Maggie held on to the heavy lavender bowl with extreme care.

*Creak, creak.* Each step made a weird noise. Jacqueline stepped on a spider. "Eee-yuuuu." She jumped and clung to Tasha. Three little rugs sat on the floor in a circle in front of Grammy Apple's purple trunk. There was also a small round mat in the center of the rugs. Maggie didn't even raise her eyebrows. She set the lavender bowl down on the round mat with extreme care.

Jacqueline checked out the dusty nooks in the deep black shadows where who-knows-what could be lurking. She sniffed the stuffy attic smell and wrinkled her nose.

"I feel so jittery," Jacqueline said.

They settled down cross-legged on the three rugs, scrunched close together, knees touching.

"Touching makes me feel better," Tasha said. "Not so nervous."

"Me too," Jacqueline said.

"And me," Maggie said. Tasha's little bag of sand waited at her side.

Jacqueline took the silver pitcher and carefully poured the seawater into the bowl. *Slosh, slosh.* It calmed down and settled into a clear still mirror.

They held hands. Tasha squeezed Maggie's right hand firmly, and Jacqueline squeezed her left hand in a bone-crushing grip. No one spoke or shifted around.

*Scratch-scratch. Scratch-scratch-scratch.*

They glanced at each other.

"Blissful!" Maggie said. "I forgot I wanted to include him. Is it okay if we let him up?"

"Whew," Jacqueline said. "I thought it was a rat."

The girls watched Blissful scoot up the old stairs. He snuggled between Maggie and Jacqueline, flicked his tail once and didn't budge. Maggie stroked his back. "I feel so much better now that you're here, Blissie."

"Oh!" Jacqueline said. A little dog bone appeared by Blissful's face. He put his paw over it and glanced around at the girls, moving just his eyes.

"Totally magical doings," Tasha whispered.

Jacqueline shivered.

"Are you okay?" Tasha put her hand on Jacqueline's.

"Just really excited."

"Okay, here we go," Maggie said. "Our first attempt at a magic ritual." She took a little packet of salt out of her pocket. "Grammy Apple says to use it to sprinkle on our hands to cleanse our space. Wave your arms around to chase away any evil spirits." She demonstrated.

*Evil spirits like Cap'n Hatch,* Maggie thought. *Would his smirking face appear in the bowl? What if nothing happens? What if someone else's face appears in the water?* She pressed her lips together and stared into the lavender bowl. The water stayed perfectly still.

Tasha was last to sprinkle the salt on her hands. There was just a little left. She gave a final swoop around the circle with her arms.

Maggie picked up Tasha's bag of beach sand and held it high. In a voice as clear as a meadowlark's song she said, "With this sand we ask for clues about the signs at the restaurant."

They each sprinkled a little sand into the lavender bowl and waited while it sank.

"So Mote It Be," Maggie said. "Remember, that means 'May It Happen' in magic talk."

"So Mote It Be," Tasha and Jacqueline repeated.

Maggie was so pleased to hear their serious tone. They were all into it!

They each peered into the shimmering bowl. The mirror of seawater shifted ever so slightly.

"All I see is sand," Jacqueline said.

"Me too. No, wait. There's something." Maggie leaned in. "Two wiggling letters. *C*, I think. And maybe an *H*. And a purple straw hat. Like your mother's, Jacqueline," Maggie said, surprised. *Madame Bonnard?*

"What? I don't see anything," Jacqueline said.

Tasha whispered, "I see pointy black things like nails." She put her hand on her heart. "Oh no, really scary, feels sharp." She scrunched her eyes shut. "Oooo, I thought the salt was supposed to protect us."

Blissful swished his tail, and the honey lemon scent floated by.

Maggie heard,

> Tell Tasha . . .
> to imagine a broom . . .
> sweeping the pointy things awaaay . . .

"Think of a broom, Tasha, quick, and sweep it all away," Maggie said.

Tasha swooshed her arms over the lavender bowl. They peered again into the still seawater.

"Gone?" Maggie said.

211

"Yes. Maybe it was supposed to mean someone is nailing up another sign and we should patrol the restaurant?" Tasha said.

Maggie groaned silently. Pictures of nails were not helping.

Jacqueline had been very quiet throughout. "I still don't see anything," she said in a little voice. "Am I a failure at magic? What am I doing wrong?"

"Nothing. Nothing," Maggie said. "My mom warned me it doesn't always work. Keep staring at it, Jacqueline. Don't worry if you don't see anything this time."

"Oh, does this count? I see a long skinny triangle. It could be the Eiffel Tower in Paris! You're both coming to Paris to visit me. Yaaaaay!" She clapped her hands over her mouth. "Oops, sorry. Got excited."

What looked like the Eiffel Tower to Jacqueline looked like a long-handled axe to Maggie. Still, it wasn't the specific evidence against Cap'n Hatch she had hoped to see.

*Grammy Apple, what are you trying to show us?* The *C* could be Carlotta, and the *H* could be Hatch, but what about the purple hat? Surely Grammy Apple wasn't pointing her in the direction of Madame Bonnard!

Blissful stuck his paw right into the lavender bowl. The water went dark.

To Maggie from Tasha

This is an invitation to a Midnight Moon Gathering. I'm writing it out in silver ink because it has to do with moonlight.

Please come to a
MAGICAL MOTHER
AND DAUGHTER GATHERING
UNDER THE FULL MOON.
Come with your mom (organized by my mom and her friend Ariana)
The fourth Tuesday in August at midnight (!!)
On Sconset Beach by the dunes
P.S. I've invited Jacqueline and her mom too. Lots of my mom's friends are coming with their daughters and grandmothers.
Love, Tasha

# CHAPTER 33

# Maggie's Father Does a Turnaround

Maggie clutched the invitation. *Please, please, Grammy Apple. If you can, make my mom want to be there with me.* Maggie left the invitation on the kitchen table for her mom to see.

Outside by the linden tree she started to sketch the sunflowers that reached way above the fence. They were so yellow, and the flowers were the size of plates. She had plenty of great drawings for the art fair, but you never knew if the next one might be THE masterpiece.

She looked around for Corby, who was supposed to meet her by the linden tree. He said he wanted to draw Maggie's house with the widow's walk on the roof. Was it her imagination, or was Corby avoiding her lately? He didn't show up for art class this week, and he's not here now. He's not sick because she had seen him racing along the wharf on his skateboard with Henri. *Oh well, he's just a kid,* she thought.

Maggie heard loud voices coming through the screen door in the kitchen. She crept over to where she could hear better. She hid behind the tall blue cornflowers, Blissful at her heels.

"Violet," her father said. "Do you realize your daughter has been invited to meet up at midnight with crazy people who call themselves magical?" He waved the Midnight Moon Gathering invitation at Maggie's mother. "Do you know anything about this? And what is that thing she wears around her neck?" Her father was now hollering.

"It's a linden tree necklace, Paul, and it belonged to my mother. Don't you remember? Maggie likes to wear it now."

"Well, I want to show you this. Somebody sneaked up to the restaurant again in the middle of the night."

He held up another sign. Maggie saw him punch his finger at every word as he read it out loud.

Evil bad people own
this place

Related to the witch
Grammy Apple

"Oh no, Blissie," Maggie said. She brushed aside the cornflowers and peered into the kitchen. She wanted to see that sign.

Blissful's tail went up in anger mode. He bared his teeth. *Grrrrrrrrr.*

"Not again. I'm so sorry, Paul," her mother said. "You must be upset. I am too."

"This isn't funny anymore, Violet." He slumped down on a kitchen chair. "Business is dropping off.

Silly witch talk must be spreading around town like an out-of-control brushfire. A reporter from the Nantucket newspaper called me and asked if he could interview me for a story about the witch signs! I said NO. I couldn't even tell him who is putting them up." He slapped the sign down on the kitchen table. "These nutsy people your daughter wants to be friends with must have something to do with this."

"How is that possible, Paul? Why would those people put up signs about witches? They're sort of witches themselves. Good witches, that is. Like Grammy Apple."

"No offense, Violet, but like I've said, your mother was a little nuts. Claiming to make things happen with magic. NOT NORMAL."

"Be that as it may, Paul. These women are friends of Tasha's mother, who you know is a respectable businesswoman. You buy flowers from her shop for the restaurant. I know some of the other women too. Mary Pepple, who happens to be a police-woman. Elsie Smithson, a real estate lawyer in town. Not exactly sketchy characters. They're planning a mother-daughter full moon gathering on the beach, which I think is very sweet. What's the harm of a little get-together around a fire on the beach? It sounds really nice to me. A bonding time with Maggie."

Maggie hugged Blissful. "I think Mom is coming! And wow, Blissie, I'm in good company. Tasha's mom and all those other people are witches too." She had no idea there were people in town who called themselves magical—even witches! "So far I think I'm the youngest witch among them, Blissie."

She crept a little closer to the kitchen window and saw her father stand up. "I won't have Maggie anywhere near that hocus-pocus." He shook his finger in the air, and his voice boomed like a loud hoot owl.

"Well, nevertheless, I'm thinking of going to the full moon gathering with Maggie. I don't see any harm in it. Tasha invited us, and I know Maggie would love to go with me," she said, keeping her voice calm.

Maggie rubbed the white patch on Blissful's head. He stopped growling.

"What is this? Halloween all year round?" Maggie's father said. He sniffed the air. Twice. "Well, your kooky mother would be happy." He sniffed again. "What's that smell? Lemons?" His voice softened. "I guess those ladies couldn't have anything to do with the signs."

Maggie held her breath. "Blissie, thanks for signaling Grammy Apple. Looks like she has decided to let him smell the honey and lemon peel. He's changing his mind!"

She heard her father say, "Oh, go on to the midnight gathering with Maggie and have fun."

"We intend to." Maggie's mom said. She gave Maggie's dad a hug.

"Hey," her father said, "there's that smell again." He took in a longer snuffle of air. "What is it?"

"It's Grammy Apple, Paulie. Don't you remember how she used to smell?" Her mother grinned at him. "Honey and lemon peel, like linden tree flowers."

She continued smiling, then waved her hand at the tall blue cornflowers outside the screen door where Maggie and Blissful were crouching.

## CHAPTER 34

# P. J. and Ben's Really Cool Plan

"Shsssssh," P. J. whispered to Ben. They crept up to the front of Chez Paul. The restaurant was dark. They listened, looked around—nobody in sight. The moon was just a sliver and gave off very little light at this late hour. P. J. hoped this middle-of-the-night adventure was going to pay off. Ben was sleeping over, and it hadn't been easy for them to sneak out of the house after bedtime. They had a plan, a surefire way to catch Cap'n Hatch in the act of putting up another sign.

Since Maggie and P. J.'s spying escapade on Cap'n Hatch and the Carlotta person behind the restaurant had led to nothing but stupid lovey-doveys between Cap'n Hatch and his lady friend, P. J. came up with a new knockout idea.

"Listen to this, Ben. Let's surprise Maggie. We catch old Cap'n Hatch right in the act of putting up a sign. With a camera on a trip wire hidden at the entrance to the restaurant! Supercool, right? We set it on a timer to work after midnight, when the restaurant is empty."

"Now you're talkin', P. J.!" Ben said.

They had pestered the salesman at the electronics store to show them how to concoct a device with a hidden camera on a timer. They kept asking questions until they completely understood how to set it up.

"What do you want this for, boys?" the store manager had asked. "Nothing against the law, I hope."

"No, no," P. J. had said. "We promise. It's a surprise for my dad."

P. J. and Ben pooled their allowance money to buy the hidden camera and wires they would need. "This is a lot of months of allowance money. It better be worth it. It was tricky to put together." P. J. said.

"And we did it! It's totally worth it!" Ben said. "When anybody touches the fence, *click*! We'll have an instant picture of the person with the sign. And he won't even know it." Ben gave P. J. a high five.

They examined the entrance to Chez Paul. Where to install the trip wire and the camera? "How about here," P. J. suggested, keeping his voice quiet. He directed his flashlight to a clump of bushes.

"Ben, are you sure it will catch anybody sneaking up from any direction?"

"We can tilt it up so it catches his face."

"The thing is," P. J. said, "we don't know what night he might be coming."

"We'll just have to check it every single night until it hits," Ben said.

"Let the spying begin!" P. J. hit Ben with another high five, a strong handshake and pats on the back.

"Aw-right!" Ben said.

The next morning Maggie propped her bike against the wide elm tree in front of her parents' restaurant and ran inside. Mmm. The fragrance of her mother's freshly baked brownies (with extra chocolate chips) floated around the big stainless-steel kitchen. It was a Mommy smell.

The chefs hadn't arrived yet to prepare the day's menu. Maggie couldn't wait to make delicious white Moon Marshmallows for the moon gathering. It was fun to be in the restaurant kitchen alone with her mom. Maggie felt important.

"Go poke your head in your father's office, Maggie."

She ran in. One of the drawings in her *Dune Grasses Doing Backbends* series looked down at her. And in a fancy driftwood frame too. All those upside-down U shapes hung right over her father's desk. Her heart fluttered with happiness. Her father's desk. There was no other place on earth she wanted her painting to hang. She read the note taped to the wall next to her drawing.

Dear Maggie,
    I would like to take photos of each of your drawings you are bringing to the art fair and put them together in an album for our family to enjoy. Before you sell them all! Can we do this together?
    Love, Daddy

Her mother came up behind her and ruffled her hair. "See?"

Maggie grinned at her mom, who tied a long white chef's apron around Maggie's waist. Maggie closed her eyes for a few seconds and breathed in these wonderful moments. She couldn't wait to tell Maggie One that her father had hung Maggie's painting of the dune grasses over his desk.

"So, we're making some fluffy marshmallows? Round? Like the moon?" Her mother formed her fingers into a circle. They peered at the recipe clipped to a rack over their workstation, and their pastry-chef hats collided. Her mom laughed. Her mom was laughing a whole bunch more lately.

"Okay," her mom said. "I'll show you how to use a candy thermometer. Let's put the honey and a little water in this saucepan. Go ahead, Maggie, you do it."

Maggie measured out the ingredients and stirred them in the pan.

"Fasten the candy thermometer on the inside."

Cap'n Hatch zoomed into Maggie's mind and made her hand tremble. The thermometer slipped.

"Oops, that's okay, Maggie," her mom said. "Now it cooks for a bit."

Cap'n Hatch here, Cap'n Hatch there. She just couldn't stop picturing him lurking around and spying on her. Maggie turned on the electric mixer and watched the grains of gelatin disappear into the swirls of water.

"What a team." Her mom took the saucepan of melted sugar syrup off the heat with care. The syrup shot up. "Hot! Now pour this sugar syrup into the mixer with your gelatin. That's right. Keep mixing until it thickens. Shall we make them lemon or vanilla?"

"Both!" Maggie divided the thickened fluff in half. "I love cooking with you, Mommy."

Her mom blew her a kiss and put a few drops of vanilla extract in one half of the mooshy, sticky marshmallow mix.

Maggie slid a lemon up and down the lemon grater, then put the lemon zest in the second batch.

"Perfect," they said together.

"Maggie, I want to tell you something." Her mother sighed. "I don't mean this with any disrespect to your father, but you need to continue to speak up when he teases you."

Her mom looked so serious.

"It's okay, Maggie. Don't let him hurt your feelings and then keep it all inside. Your father can take it. He loves us, and he knows we love him."

Maggie smiled. "Thanks, Mommy. Really, thanks. But I'm feeling supergood about Daddy right now." Since the riptide there hadn't been one single "toothpick legs" comment from her father or anything else hurtful.

Maggie set out two baking sheets her mom had lined with plastic wrap.

"Scrape the marshmallow mixture onto the baking sheets, and we'll let it sit for a while. Then we'll make moon circles with a cookie cutter."

Her mom pulled a copper skillet off the rack. "How about making one huge chocolate-chip cookie while we wait for the marshmallows to set?"

"We can bring it to Dad and P. J.," Maggie said. "And could we bake another one for Ben for the clambake this weekend?" Ben's face and red hair popped into Maggie's mind. She felt herself blushing . . . again.

Maggie picked right up on the twinkle in her mother's eyes.

"Sure," her mom said.

## CHAPTER 35

# What Can Happen Under a Full Moon?

**M**aggie walked with her mom along the moonlit beach toward a flickering bonfire ahead, cuddled in by the night. It was nearly midnight, a thrilling hour to be up and about.

*Crash, whooooosh.* The high waves and big swoops of the beach were drenched in pale-yellow moonlight. *What's the right word for how I feel?* She inhaled the salty air. *I know, 'enchanted.' I feel enchanted. Like I'm breathing in air that is full of magic.* And even better, she was here with her mom, their arms linked. The rough sand tickled the bottoms of her feet. A Midnight Moon Gathering! Just for mothers and daughters! And grandmothers and granddaughters. What was it going to be like?

"I wish Grammy Apple could be here, Mommy," Maggie said.

"Well, you never know," her mom said with a twinkle in her eyes.

Everyone arrived with baskets of food. Maggie set their box of Moon Marshmallows on a blanket with all the other goodies. She peeked under a napkin. Chocolate whoopee pies! Four covered pitchers labeled "Midnight Peppermint Tea" sat in a bucket of ice.

Maggie ran to find Tasha down the beach.

"Hey, Maggie, look. A baby starfish. I don't believe it. It's perfect, all pink and white. I'll save it."

"Wow, cool."

Tasha turned over a small white clamshell with her toe. "Hey, let's collect these for a memory of tonight."

They scoured the moonlit beach and collected tiny shells.

"Ugh. Here's a captain's toenail shell," Tasha said.

"Pick it up. It's lu-mi-ne-scent," Maggie said. "That means 'shiny,' I think."

"I know, but when I think of the name it looks totally disgusting. A captain's thick old yellow toenail."

Maggie grabbed it and pretended to put it on her tongue.

"Eee-yuuuu, ga-ross, Maggie."

Maggie threw it down on the sand, and they both started laughing.

*We're really, truly best friends forever again,* Maggie thought.

"Tasha! Maggie!" Tasha's mother called out.

They ran back to the fire with their stash of shells.

Jacqueline arrived with her mother. "I'm putting my very best piece of seaweed by the fire. For good luck. It's the kind you pop with your fingers, but please don't pop it." She carefully laid the seaweed on a piece of driftwood. Others had put their treasures around the bright fire: a seagull feather, three perfect pieces of green sea glass and the black shell of a horseshoe crab. Tasha laid the baby starfish she had just found next to Jacqueline's seaweed on the piece of driftwood. "A moon offering," she said to Jacqueline.

The small fire crackled in the night air and made their cheeks warm when they got close to it. Maggie's mother draped Grammy Apple's linden tree necklace across two white stones. Maggie could almost feel it breathing.

"Grammy Apple. She's here," Maggie said in a hushed voice.

Her mother brushed Maggie's hair back. "Yes, she's here."

With a nod from a lady with long silver hair, everyone found a place and spread their blankets in a big circle around the fire. Maggie settled in between her mom and Tasha.

"That's Ariana," Tasha told her. "She organized this with my mom. Isn't she beautiful? Like she comes from some enchanted place or something? That's her daughter over there and her granddaughter."

"You know that word 'enchanted'?" Maggie asked Tasha. "I just thought of it, too, for this whole beach at night. When I was walking here with my mom."

The moonlight glowed down on Ariana's face. Maggie thought she had such a kind smile. Someone handed Ariana a flickering candle.

Maggie pulled her hoodie closer around her, cozy and excited down to her bones.

"Welcome, welcome to all the mothers and daughters and granddaughters gathered here on this full moon night." Maggie snuggled closer to her mother.

Tasha's mother walked around the circle with a large basket and offered each mother a candle in a holder. She lit the candles one by one with a long match. It looked like a wand. The moonlight mingled with the flickering candles that formed a circle of yellow shimmers. Maggie had never seen anything so heavenly in her whole life.

"You are all very beautiful in the glow of the moonlight," Ariana said. "This is the Harvest Moon, the closest to the earth of all the full moons. We are especially close to our maternal ancestors tonight, our mothers, grandmothers, great-grandmothers and way back in time to forever. Perhaps you can feel some of them."

Maggie felt a gentle breeze float between and around her and her mother. "I don't smell honey and lemon peel," she said to her mother. "Do you think that means Grammy Apple is with us even without the smell sometimes?"

"Yes, Maggie, I think that's just what it means."

Ariana's voice floated in the moonlight, a soft melody. Maggie closed her eyes. It sounded like music escaping from a harp, a mermaid's harp. She saw the mermaid in her mind. She would draw her.

"We all have a wish or dream to give to our daughters," Ariana said. "As we go around the circle, each mother will give her daughter or granddaughter her wish and then pass the candle to her."

Ariana turned to a little girl on her right, about five years old. "To Gwennie, my extraordinary granddaughter. May your astonishing connections to the living creatures on Nantucket deepen and bring you and your animal friends many happy times together."

Gwennie took the candle from her grandmother and piped up. "Um. I just want to say that next week, I think, after this full moon, there will be lots and lots of jellyfish kissing. And then the jellyfish will be mommies. Like the mommies here. And baby jellyfish will come. Isn't that nice?"

Ariana beamed. "A little future witch."

Jacqueline's mother and Tasha's mother both told their wishes to their daughters and passed their candles to them. Maggie watched and barely heard the others while she was waiting for her mother's turn.

Here it was. Everyone was quiet. The woodsy smell from the fire and the fragrance of the salty sea floated through her. Maggie's mother reached for her hand. "With this candle, my sweet Maggie, I want to give you two gifts. I want to give you the gift of yourself. You are deeply loved by all of us for who you are." She touched Maggie's cheek. "And here's my second gift, Maggie. Because of you I now realize that my own mother, your Grammy Apple, has been using her magic to help you feel happy with yourself and accept the wonderful magic you hold inside. And to bring out the artist in you. Now I can love her without any bad feelings. Thank you, my very special girl." She handed Maggie the candle, and Maggie put her head on her mother's shoulder. She felt as if everyone in the circle were hugging them.

"And now for a very special moment," Ariana said. "Sometimes, if we're lucky, we might wake up in the morning with a special name for ourselves in our heads. A name that seems just right."

She nodded at Maggie, Tasha and Jacqueline.

"Three of our girls have chosen their magic names. They would like to share them," Ariana said.

Jacqueline walked forward. Maggie nodded to Tasha, and they both got up at the same time, holding on to their candles. Her heart had been so filled tonight. Was there room for more?

"Go ahead, Maggie," Tasha said.

"No, you start."

Tasha glanced around the circle, resting her eyes for a moment on each person. "My magic name is Butterfly because I followed one around once with my camera. The pictures came out great." In a shy voice she added, "And not everybody can do that."

"Hello to Butterfly," the group said.

Maggie nodded to Jacqueline.

"My magic name is Nantucket, because this is where my truly best friends live and where I almost drowned. But now I'm not afraid to go back in the water, sort of. Also, it's where you find the best seaweed."

"Hello to Nantucket," the group said.

Maggie stepped forward. "My magic name is Luna Linden because when I look up into the linden tree where I put the mirrors, I know I want to draw pictures forever." She felt her cheeks flush and looked down at her feet. "I know now that I am an artist."

She turned to her mother. "And Luna means 'moon.' I added that part just tonight because I see the full moon connecting my Grammy Apple's heart to my mother's heart and then to my heart."

"Hello to Luna Linden," the group said.

Maggie's happy feelings were hopping all over the beach, and the ocean air smelled like midnight. For her, nobody in the world existed at this moment except these wonderful people. Not even Cap'n Hatch.

"Time to roast the Moon Marshmallows," Maggie said. Her mind flashed to the restaurant kitchen and mixing up the marshmallows with her mom. She went over to her mom and gave her a big hug.

"And eat chocolate whoopee pies," Tasha said.

By two o'clock in the morning the magical gathering began to break up. Maggie pulled her hoodie tight against the wind that was beginning to make her shiver. Someone had extinguished the fire, and everyone scattered off in various directions home.

Maggie's mom rubbed Maggie's cold hands with her warm ones. "Better now?" They walked arm in arm down the beach toward the road and the car.

Maggie looked straight up into the round, butter-yellow full moon. Moonbeam after moonbeam fell into Maggie's heart. Suddenly, a sharp fear swelled up inside her again. Cap'n Hatch. She couldn't keep her secret bound up in there a second longer. Big sobs tumbled out from deep down in her chest. She wanted to tell her mother absolutely everything about Cap'n Hatch. And she was going to. Right this minute.

Maggie spilled the whole horrible story, how he bragged to her that he had big secrets on his computer in code, how he would tell everyone the Greenleafs were wicked witches like Grammy Apple if Maggie dared tell anyone.

"The witch signs are all my fault," she sobbed. "I told P. J. about Cap'n Hatch, that he had even waved an axe at me." She stopped and sobbed even deeper. "And Cap'n Hatch found out. I didn't dare tell you or Dad. Cap'n Hatch would tell all the kids in school I was a witch, even though I'm glad I'm a witch like Grammy Apple, and nobody would come to Daddy's restaurant." More sobs and gulps. "Cap'n Hatch must be the person putting up the witch signs in the middle of the night."

Her mother dropped her backpack and held her close. "Shh. It's okay. It's okay, Maggie." They were quiet for a moment, and Maggie's crying began to calm down. Her mom shook her head. "But I don't understand Cap'n Hatch. He loved Grammy Apple."

Maggie whispered through tears, "He has some secret. He doesn't want anyone to know anything about him, Mommy, I'm telling you."

"How dare he threaten you! This is very bad." Her voice rose. "He's going to hear from me."

Maggie couldn't believe the relief running through her now that she told her mother about Cap'n Hatch. She felt safer and a trillion times better.

## CHAPTER 36

# The Art Fair, Yaaaaay

Maggie's mom told her she and her dad had tried twice to catch Cap'n Hatch on his boat, but so far, no luck. She told Maggie they would search him out relentlessly until they confronted him face-to-face.

But today was the art fair, so phooey on Cap'n Hatch, Maggie thought. She was so excited she had to keep from twirling round and round.

"Mom. You're driving really slowly. Can't you hurry?" She smoothed the ruffles on Jacqueline's skirt from Paris. She was glad she had dressed up for the occasion.

Finally! Her big day was here. Maggie wondered if her drawings would stand up next to the grown-ups' artwork. She pinched herself. This was not a dream. Maggie had one hour to put fishnet on the inside walls of her open pop-up tent and arrange and hang her drawings.

Twenty-five pop-up tents sat next to each other in rows on the grassy meadow by the harbor, each one assigned by Mrs. Droop to a specific artist. Maggie's mom swung the car over to Maggie's section. Maggie found her name on the second tent in from the entrance. One of the best spots!

Exhibitors bustled around their tents. Maggie glimpsed small oil paintings of seascapes, a big sculpture of a mermaid and lots of model sailboats of all sizes. And lots of grown-ups.

"Do you still want me to drop you off and come back later?" her mom asked.

"Yes, thanks." Maggie didn't want any help arranging her drawings. Maggie One had offered to help her too. But Maggie had such a clear picture in her mind of how she wanted to display her drawings. She would arrange them so that the color, size or subject of each picture would enhance the one next to it. Like maybe all the drawings of Blissie in a row, so it would look like he was moving. Her mom thought she was old enough to do this by herself, and her mom was right.

Maggie dropped her heavy portfolio on the long table in front of her tent. It was stuffed with her drawings, all beautifully matted. Her mom had helped her with that. She held up one of Blissie rolling in the sand. She looked at it hard. It's good! A tidal wave of little thrills rose up inside her.

Maggie reached into her backpack and pulled out a pale-blue tablecloth, a fishnet, a money box, lots of clothespins for clipping up her drawings, her starfish, a jar of beach sand, some shells and her name sign—everything she needed to create Maggie's World in her tent.

With the help of a step stool she found by one of the tents, she took the clothespins and clipped her matted drawings onto the fishnet, taking care to make them secure. She stepped down to make sure she liked the overall effect.

"Hmm . . . I think I'll put my starfish in between some of the drawings. And Jacqueline's clump of seaweed by the acrobatic seagull. I'd better. Jacqueline would be hurt if I didn't hang her seaweed."

All of her drawings together! For one extraordinary moment she saw herself grown-up, standing in front of her own exhibit in a big art gallery in Boston or New York City, maybe even Paris.

Mrs. Droop bustled from tent to tent. "Beautiful pottery! Original landscapes! How creative you all are." She beamed her wide, toothy smile at Maggie, who was setting up her smaller drawings on miniature artist easels on the table in front of her tent.

"Your display is dazzling! I knew I was right to find you for the art fair, dear," Mrs. Droop said.

*Find me! Not hardly,* she thought. *It was Grammy Apple's honey and lemon peel that opened your eyes.*

"Thank you, Mrs. Droop. I hope people like them and that I sell a lot."

If nobody came to her tent, she would be so embarrassed.

People meandered in all at once, and in a moment there were crowds. Her heart was fluttering like a butterfly as she adjusted Tasha's small photo of herself drawing under the linden tree. She smoothed out the sand she had sprinkled on her long blue tablecloth and rearranged the shells around her sign.

## ARTWORK BY MAGGIE EVA ELIZABETH COTTLE GREENLEAF

"May I see that collage up closer, please? The tree?" a woman asked. There were several other people peering at her drawings.

Maggie's large collage of the linden tree with the mirrors sparkled in the middle of the fishnet wall. Her heart-shaped tissue paper leaves fluttered green next to little circles of silver foil that she used to represent the mirrors. The silver foil reflected the sun's rays now peeking into her tent. Maggie thought the very best parts of her collage were the ripples of brown corrugated paper she used for the trunk and branches. It was three feet high and two feet wide.

Maggie smiled and unclipped the big collage from the fishnet. She handed it to the woman. *Show her Tasha's photo!* "This is what the real tree looks like with the mirrors," Maggie said in her most pleasant voice. "I named my collage *The Fairy-Tale Tree*. I'm asking twenty-five dollars for it."

The woman stared at Maggie's collage for a few seconds longer. "Well, it looks like it popped right out of a fairy tale," the woman said. Maggie stood perfectly still, holding her lips in a nice smile. Did she look too anxious?

"I'll take it," the woman said. "Would you throw in the little photo too? I can't believe this was done by someone your age." She handed Maggie a twenty-dollar bill and five one-dollar bills. Maggie clipped the little photo to the collage. She felt a momentary tinge of regret as the woman took her collage from her hands forever.

"Thank you so much," Maggie said. "I hope you enjoy it." She waved goodbye to the lady and her glittering collage. *A stranger loved my linden tree enough to pay money for it. My very first sale in my life!*

Quite a few people were stopping by her tent, not just glancing and whizzing by either. They were lingering. Plus, she had several actual buyers, and the fair was only half over.

Maggie felt something pulling on her flip-flop under the table. Blissful? But she hadn't brought Blissful. She yanked her foot back, knelt down and lifted up the long blue tablecloth.

"Henri!" she hissed. What—are—you—*doing*—here?"

"Just a joke, Maggie! Ha-ha." He crept out from under the table and ran off.

Maggie popped up. *Annoying child, that Henri.* A man asked about her acrobatic seagulls. "Yes, I drew those earlier this summer. Um, from my imagination."

She had no time to get irritated with Henri. Her tent was busy with people, and here came Maggie One heading over to Maggie's booth. Maggie smiled at her and stopped herself from jumping up and down. That would be so unbusinesslike.

"Wow, I'm proud of you, Maggie Two," Maggie One said. She touched a drawing. "This was always my favorite of yours." She walked away with the drawing *Blissful Tangled Up in Seaweed.* Maggie wouldn't let her pay for it.

Wait. She stared in disbelief. A pointed black witch hat sat on the end of her table. Maggie grabbed it so fast she almost knocked over her sign. She stuck it under the table, willing her tears back. How mortifying to cry. She looked quickly from left to right for Cap'n Hatch.

"Yes, sir," she returned to a customer. "That pastel is Brant Point Lighthouse, and the flowers are honeysuckle."

Her eyes darted around. Where was Cap'n Hatch?

"I'll take it. You make the lighthouse look flat. So different from most drawings of lighthouses," the man said.

"Thank you so much."

Maggie One came back and bought two more drawings. P. J. and Ben came by with disappointing news. Nothing had turned up on the camera they had planted.

"P. J.," Maggie said in a low voice. "Someone left a black witch hat here on my table. I'm stepping on it right now."

"Well, it's not Cap'n Hatch. I heard he's out fishing all day," P. J. said.

"That's not possible, not possible at all." Her mind was whirling. "Maybe Cap'n Hatch told someone else to put a witch hat by my tent? Carlotta?"

P. J. and Ben both shook their heads. "That's a little far-fetched, Maggie. She's probably with him. I have to admit, the culprit could be another person entirely." P. J. kept his voice low.

"Another person? But who else would do such a mean thing?" Maggie hissed.

## CHAPTER 37

# Maggie's Big Moment

Later that afternoon, Maggie's mirrors in the linden tree sparkled down on the lively group that had gathered in her backyard to celebrate her wonderful success at the art fair.

Grown-ups had paid money for her drawings! The funny posing sandpiper, Blissful and his sillies, all got snatched up.

Her mother announced, "Maggie sold seventeen drawings. Seventeen! And her beautiful linden tree collage sold during the first seven minutes." She turned to Maggie One. "I kind of hated to see that one go. I would have liked it for our living room."

Her father was standing on the sidelines, beaming a proud smile over to Maggie. She smiled back, so happy for the loving feelings that flowed back and forth between them. She had finally had the guts to speak up, and her dad's upsetting comments had mostly stopped. And when he slipped and said something hurtful, Maggie just opened her eyes wide and willed the comment to bounce back off her. It was working every time. Without Grammy Apple. By herself.

Maggie took in the happy scene around her, still astounded by people's reactions to her work at the art fair.

"Technically perfect," one woman said.

"Fresh, bright colors," said another.

And the best, "An original take on shorebirds— and dogs."

She remembered only one uncomplimentary remark. A woman had strolled by Maggie's booth, looked at Maggie's drawing of a sailboat and said to her friend, "Her perspective is way off." They had walked away.

Thinking about this woman now, in the midst of her party and well-wishers, a moment of self-doubt flared up. But Maggie squashed it immediately. *That's how I saw the boat, and that's what counts.*

She waved to Jacqueline and Madame Bonnard, Corby and Henri. The twins were stuffing their mouths with red velvet cupcakes. There was Tasha and her mom and Ariana! Was Ben here? Maggie greeted the kids in her art class. "That was so nice to see you all walking over to my tent together," Maggie said to them. The whole group had shown up at the fair. "Please help yourselves to some cherry lemonade. And my mom's red velvet cupcakes."

Ben cupped his hands around his mouth and shouted, "She was awesome, everybody!"

Maggie's tummy did a little flip-flop.

"Wahoo," said Maggie One. She held Maggie's drawing *Blissful Tangled Up in Seaweed* up high.

"To Maggie!"

Maggie saw a blur of raised glasses of cherry lemonade. Big red cherries bobbed on top of the lemonade in her honor. She clapped and grinned and grinned.

Then a man stepped out from behind the tool-shed. Her heart stopped. Maggie stared. *No, he wouldn't dare show up here after all his threats to me.*

Cap'n Hatch. With that Carlotta lady. Then he did an extraordinary thing. He tipped his baseball cap at Maggie and gave her a warm, grandfatherly smile. It wiped away all the grouchy lines on his face.

*What am I supposed to think? Right now, he doesn't look like anyone who would put up mean signs.* But the image of his axe floated in front of her.

Something inside Maggie went *ker-klunk*.

A big knot squeezed the inside of her stomach. She reminded herself that real gumption meant doing what you had to do even when your stomach was squeezing. Especially when your stomach was squeezing.

*Just step right up and make an announcement.*
*She would do it.*

Maggie pushed past her guests. "Excuse me, I'm sorry, excuse me." She pushed into the middle of the crowd and climbed up on a tree stump. She touched the ruffles on her Paris skirt and slipped her hand in the pocket where she had once put Grammy Apple's letter for courage. She felt a surge of confidence without the letter.

"Hey, everybody," she said, waving her hand up high. "I'm happy you came, so thank you, but I have to bring something up." She cleared her throat. "Something horrible."

Everybody stopped munching the red velvet cupcakes. They stopped sipping their cherry lemonades. They focused on Maggie.

"Okay. So, as you may know, someone has been putting up really nasty signs in front of my father's restaurant. Stuff like, 'The Greenleafs are witches, and they poison food. Don't eat here.'"

Out of the corner of her eye Maggie saw Cap'n Hatch raise his bushy eyebrows and shift his eyes left and right.

*Ha! Does this mean he's nervous and guilty?*

Murmurs from the crowd: "Terrible." "How awful." "What's this all about?"

In a voice that was loud and as clear as a young warbler's, she said, "And fewer people are coming to the restaurant. Not to mention it's totally weird and mean of that person." She felt strong inside. Like after she had pulled Jacqueline out of the riptide. Maggie looked over at P. J., and his dropped jaw. He mouthed at her, "Wow, Maffie, that's gumption!"

"Maybe somebody here has a clue to track this person down," Maggie continued, trying not to focus on Cap'n Hatch, because maybe it wasn't him. She stood up taller and squared her shoulders. "I say, if they are here, they should step up and confess." She squinted her eyes and peered at Cap'n Hatch. She couldn't help it.

"Ahem. Harrumph." Cap'n Hatch came forward and took two steps toward Maggie. He was close.

*Oh no, he's going to pounce,* she thought.

He loomed over her, then stepped back and tugged at his baseball cap with the boat on it.

"Harrumph," he said, gazing down at Maggie. "Maggie thinks I put up the signs. I did not. 'Twasn't me."

*Is he lying?*

"I don't blame you, Maggie. I made you promise not to tell my secret. Then I was sorry I told you anything about having a secret and tried to scare you every time I could. Tried to make you worry I would spread witch rumors about your family. I'm sorry. But 'twasn't me who put up the signs."

*I still can't tell if he's lying,* Maggie thought.

Cap'n Hatch turned and was all lovey-dovey with the lady standing close to his side. He took her hand.

"Here's my secret, everybody. This is Miss Carlotta Jenks from Boston. We met online. Yes, that's right. Online." He grinned. "She's my honey, and I'm going to marry her."

Miss Carlotta waved and smiled. She put her head on Cap'n Hatch's shoulder. The yellow daisy in her gray curls nestled into his fishing jacket.

Maggie frowned. *What does that have to do with putting up signs?*

"I didn't tell anyone about courting her," Cap'n Hatch said. "Didn't want you all jabbering about us getting married at our age. Eighty-one." He pointed to himself. "Eighty." He pointed to Miss Carlotta. Cap'n Hatch blushed as bright as the red cherry in his lemonade. "Didn't want you all up in my business." He frowned back at Maggie.

"So we sent love notes back and forth online through secret pictures of my dog, Scupper. Harrumph. Steganography, you know."

Maggie didn't know what to feel. This was so confusing. If not him, who? Not knowing was almost scarier than believing it was Cap'n Hatch.

"Now Carlotta's said yes, and you can all jabber as much as you want." Cap'n Hatch gave Miss Carlotta Jenks a kiss on the top of her gray curls. She patted his cheek.

"So whoever you are," Cap'n Hatch shouted to the crowd, "get your behind over here and confess. If you're here. 'Tisn't right to destroy someone's business or family reputation. Besides, those signs are cockamamie nonsense. Apple wouldn't hurt a flea, witch or not. She was different. And if being different means making magic that helps people, then I say hooray for magic, and hooray for witches. Lord knows she's looked out for me all these years. Poison soup? Cockamamie nonsense."

## CHAPTER 38

# No! It Couldn't Be

**S**ilence spread over the crowd, and no one budged. Maggie didn't move or breathe. Her eyes were riveted on Cap'n Hatch. She just knew he was telling the truth. It sounded right. It felt right. She had been so wrong, so stubborn, even though he did actually threaten her. But she had refused to consider in any serious way that someone else might have put up the signs.

*Real gumption would be to admit I made a mistake,* Maggie thought.

*Arf! Arf, grrrrrrrrr. ARF!*

Blissful.

*ARF! Arf, grrrrrrrrr.*

What a rumpus! Blissful darted around and around and parked himself right in front of the twins.

*Grrrrrrrr.* He nipped at their ankles and pulled on their socks.

"Hey! Cut it out," they said together. They ducked behind their mother.

*Arf! Grrrrrrrr.* Blissful found Henri's bare ankle and gave it a sharp nip.

"Aiiiiiiii!"

Maggie watched Henri pull at his baseball cap. It had a boat on it. A light clicked on inside her head. His cap from sailing camp! Corby, who was crying, didn't have a cap. The baseball cap with the boat on it, left at the scene of the restaurant fire? Corby's?

No. She felt a punch in her stomach. Wasn't Corby her little friend, always tagging after her? He told her he loved learning art things from her. He would never hurt her this way, would he?

Corby was sobbing into his mother's skirts, and Maggie choked up. She looked over at her dad's bewildered face and took a deep breath.

"I'm sorry, Madame Bonnard, but would you please ask the twins if they had anything to do with the signs? I mean, look what Blissful is doing to their socks. That's not like him."

Her mind raced. The clues *H* and *C* in the lavender bowl? Not Hatch and Carlotta. Henri and Corby? And the purple hat? Just like Madame Bonnard's. A connection to the twins?

"Aiiiiiiii!" Corby tried to shake Blissful off his ankle. "It was us," he sobbed. "Henri and me." He looked at Maggie and cried harder. "I wanted to tell you, but I was scared you would really hate me and say I can never come to art class and never say 'hi' back if I say 'hi' to you."

"WHAT?" Their mother yanked them both by their collars. Her face flushed purple, and her eyes bore into their faces, from one twin to the other. "WHAT WERE YOU THINKING?"

"It was just a joke," Henri said. His voice trembled. "Only a joke."

"We read about Grammy Apple in Jacqueline's journal," Corby said, sniffling.

"You what?" Jacqueline screamed at them.

"We just wanted to know what it was like to be out in the middle of the night, that's all," Henri said, trying to free himself from his mother's grasp and wipe away big tears.

"Are you two completely crazy in the head?" Jacqueline said, each word pounded out in fury.

"You are grounded until we leave for France. And I mean grounded," Madame Bonnard said. "In separate rooms. Such a terrible, unkind thing to do to Chef Greenleaf! I'm horrified."

Blissful continued to bite their ankles. *Grrrrrrrr. Nip, nip.*

"Ouch! Okay. Okay. It was our fault the fire on the restaurant fence got started," Henri blurted out.

The whole crowd at Maggie's party took a deep breath and stared at the twins.

"We didn't start the fire on purpose, we swear! It was dark, and we lit some matches so we could see better," Henri said. "Also, it's more my fault than Corby's. He didn't really want to do it as much as me. He wouldn't even come with me to put the witch hat on Maggie's table at the art fair. Don't blame Corby equal with me."

Corby looked at his brother. "That's okay. I thought it was fun, too, in the beginning."

Madame Bonnard addressed the crowd around the linden tree. "I'm so very ashamed for my boys. I'm dreadfully sorry." She continued to hold them both by the back of their collars. Hard.

"You will get a written apology, Chef Greenleaf, from both of them." She yanked them toward their car. "The only time you two can go out is to help Chef Greenleaf with chores. Like cleaning up and taking out garbage. If he even wants you. Do you both hear me?" The twins nodded, chins in their chests. Madame Bonnard's face darkened to a deeper purple.

She put them in the car. One in the front and one in the back with Jacqueline. Corby didn't look out at Maggie, and she heard more sobs as they pulled out of the driveway.

Blissful was barking so loudly the birds stopped chirping.

A voice in Maggie's ear made her look up to the widow's walk on the roof of her house. There was her imaginary sea captain, Jeremiah Cottle, waving at her with his spyglass. It felt so good to see a friend at this terrible moment. She didn't think he would ever betray her like Corby did.

"I was beginning to think Cap'n Hatch didn't have both oars in the water," he called down. Jeremiah Cottle tapped his finger on his forehead. "Maybe a little tetched in the head? Glad the signs were just a prank, albeit a naughty one. Not something meant to hurt." He disappeared.

Maggie's dad walked over and gave her a hug. "That was *really* brave of you, Maggie. You stood up for your family in front of everyone. That took major guts."

"It was really Blissful," Maggie said.

"He was just your assistant."

"Harrumph. Lookee here, Maggie-girl." Cap'n Hatch approached them, trying to look gruff. "If you're a little witch like your Grammy Apple, you're darn lucky. I didn't mean none of those things I did, Maggie. Apple knows I'm an old grouch. And she gave me the what-for but good. My apple tattoo burned and itched me something fierce the whole time I was scaring you."

Maggie wondered if she would ever stop being frightened of Cap'n Hatch, Carlotta or no Carlotta. She hoped so. He didn't look so scary right now.

"I thought maybe you were scaring me because Grammy Apple married Grandpa, and you decided after all this time to get back at her," Maggie said.

"Naw. All wrong. That marriage business with Apple? After feeling hurt for one week I was happy just to be her friend. She's the best friend I've ever had, up until Carlotta here." He pulled Miss Carlotta in closer and pointed to his arm. "Lookee here. My old apple tattoo is almost gone. Guess Apple knows I don't need her watching over me anymore. Got a new lady to pester me. Ha-ha."

Miss Carlotta took Maggie's hand in hers. "Maggie dear. I'm very, very sorry he scared you so for such a silly reason. He's really just a sweet kitten inside. Come visit us on the boat next week. I'm going to knit you a pretty scarf. What's your favorite color?"

"Um. Purple. Thank you." Maggie thought Miss Carlotta Jenks looked like a fresh round muffin with rosy cheeks.

"And a scarf for your Blissful." She winked and leaned down to pet him. He let her.

## CHAPTER 39

# The Famous Greenleaf Clambake

"Hey, Dad, can I help you dig the firepit for the clambake this year?" Maggie asked.

The annual Greenleaf clambake on the beach got bigger every summer. More friends and more lobsters. Maggie and her dad were by the dunes searching for a good spot for digging.

"It's pretty heavy work, Maggie-girl." He grinned at her. "But anybody who can make it out of a riptide can dig a little hole on the beach." Her dad took one of the two big shovels on his shoulders and handed it to Maggie. He made a silly motion with his two index fingers, a little sign between them that they used to do when she was little. They hadn't exchanged that sign for a long time. Maggie grinned up at her dad and gave the silly sign back.

Her father put his hands on her shoulders and looked into Maggie's eyes. "When you stood up in the middle of the crowd at your party and challenged whoever put up those miserable signs to come forward—" Her dad's voice caught. "I was never so proud of anyone in my whole life. You are a special, strong girl, and I love you very, very much."

Maggie closed her eyes and let her father's words nestle in the place in her heart that had been waiting for them for a long time.

They dug the hole almost two feet down. Blissful did his bit by scattering the sand around at high speed. Sometimes he pushed some of it back in the hole. They laughed and laughed.

"Done," he said. "Let's line this big pit with the rocks I stacked in the dunes."

They worked together quickly, piled wood logs on the rocks and lit the fire.

"Now we wait about an hour," her dad said. He poked at the logs with a long stick. They were beginning to catch and flame up. "Lookin' good. How about a game of paddleball?"

Blissful was sitting on the rackets.

"You're on, Dad," Maggie shouted as she raced down to the hard sand by the breaking waves.

They played a long time. *Clack.* Missed! Back and forth. Running, swinging, hitting. With each swing of her racket Maggie felt more connected to her dad. No, "Good one, Toothpick!" jokes. No Skinny Merinks Merandio. Just a lot of laughing.

While her father babysat the fire, Maggie took a walk down the beach with Blissful. She picked up a small piece of driftwood and wrote in the sand:

# BEST SUMMER EVER

She leaned down and kissed Blissful. "I bet it's one of your best summers, too, right Blissie, you magical little dog?" Maggie walked back by the dunes. Her father was sitting on a blanket, looking out to sea. Maggie saw that the soft crash of the waves was making him feel content, just like she felt.

"I was thinking about Grammy Apple," her father said, as Maggie relaxed down beside him. "She showed you your gumption, and your gumption showed me how teasing hurts." He nodded toward a big flat rock, a distance away from the fire. There was the album with the photos of her drawings she and her father had put together, sitting on top for all their guests to see.

P. J. and Ben arrived with Maggie's mom. They lugged a basket full of potatoes down the dunes. They ran back up to the car for the crate of squirming black lobsters and another filled with cherrystone clams. Maggie's mom set a vase of linden tree flowers on a flat piece of driftwood by the dune steps to welcome the guests with the soft scent of honey and lemon peel. Maggie smiled. Linden tree flowers stopped blooming by July, and this was the beginning of September. But Maggie's, Grammy Apple's and Blissful's magical ones were in full bloom.

A few guests began to show up. There was Maggie One coming down the dune steps. Maggie looked twice. She was wearing a tall, pointed black witch hat. Cap'n Hatch walked slowly behind her down the dunes with Miss Carlotta on his arm. Both had on witch hats.

*What?* Maggie stared.

A crowd of friends and townspeople arrived, all in witch hats. Tasha and her parents, Jacqueline and her mother, all walked down the dunes in witch hats. Everyone was greeted by the honey lemon peel scent coming from the linden flowers in the vase by the path.

Maggie couldn't help herself. Arms up high, she spun around and around. She would have hugged everybody if she could. Instead she just said, "Wow."

The kids from Maggie's art class carried a big banner. It said,

## WE LOVE MAGIC

"I'm flabbergasted," Maggie's dad said. "Come over here, Greenleafs. I want to talk to you." He motioned everyone, including Blissful, to gather round him, away from the arriving guests.

"Okay, I'm convinced. Grammy Apple's magic is real. And you know what? Her magic is all about love. I feel it, and so does the whole town, it seems." He chuckled. "Those people who boycotted the restaurant? Tourists!" He gathered his family in closer. "All right. Family hug." Honey and lemon peel smells wafted around them, mighty strong.

He picked up a stray witch hat and put it on Maggie's head. She looked up at her dad. She didn't need him to say anything. That gesture said it all.

The beach enclosed the happy guests in a cocoon of salty sea air mixed with the fragrance of the clambake. Someone was flying a kite with a long green tail. And there was Maggie One, poring over the album of Maggie's drawings and paintings. She smiled over at Maggie and hugged the album to her chest.

"Maggie." Jacqueline's mom pulled her aside and gave her two big envelopes. "From Corby and Henri. They made these for you on their own. I had nothing to do with it, and I must confess I melted when I saw them." She touched Maggie's cheek. "I think I've punished them enough. They've been very sad and sorry about what they did."

Maggie pulled out a drawing in red crayon from one of the envelopes.

> I am very, very, very sorry for the signs, and I will never be bad again on account of it hurts people. From Henri Bonnard
> This is a very strong promise.

She opened the other envelope. It was a drawing of herself and Corby in art class.

> You always smile at me. You teach me all about drawing, and also I will never forget you in Paris. I'm very sorry I was bad. From Corby Bonnard
> Also you like all my drawings.

In a quiet voice Maggie said, "Madame Bonnard, would you consider going home and bringing them to the clambake?"

"I was hoping you would say that, sweet Maggie. I'll be right back with the twins."

Maggie smiled. Everything began to feel right inside.

The clambake needed tending.

"Hey, where's my partner? C'mon Maggie, let's get this slimy seaweed on the fire." Her dad handed her the heavy oven mitts. They layered wet seaweed on top of the rocks and wood embers.

"Clumsy old mitts." Maggie laughed. They both made their silly sign with two fingers at the same time.

Maggie picked out the wiggling lobsters from the crate and arranged them in pans without so much as one *eee-yuuuu*, then lowered the pans on the white-hot fire with the corn, clams and potatoes. P. J. clapped loudly, and Ben gave her a dazzling smile.

She couldn't help touching her witch hat. She would wear it everywhere, even to school when it started in a few weeks. Well, she'd have to think about that one. Either the witch hat or Grammy Apple's floppy red one with the pink rose.

Maggie left the fire and sauntered down toward the breaking waves.

"Hey, Ben," she waved. "Come here. I have something for you."

Ben jumped up and was there in three seconds.

Maggie pulled the huge chocolate-chip cookie in plastic wrap out from under her sweatshirt. "My mom and I made it at the restaurant."

"Wow." Ben unwrapped the plastic and took a major bite. He chewed it, swallowed it and looked straight into Maggie's eyes. He planted a big chocolate-chip-cookie kiss on Maggie's cheek.

*Boom! Crash!* The sound of the surf echoed the lurches in her tummy.

She was going to faint, surely. She straightened her witch hat and managed a blush and a grin. Then she kissed him back on the cheek.

"I really like you, Maggie," Ben said. "And this cookie too. Thanks for baking it!"

They ran back to the fire together. Maggie felt a little older than she did ten minutes ago.

What a feast. They had her dad's famous bay-leaf melted butter to drizzle over the clambake. It smelled so yummy. A Greenleaf family smell.

Ben played the guitar. They all danced, witch hats bobbing up and down. Jacqueline twirled around with P. J. and Maggie One. Maggie had the twins on either side of her, bouncing to the music. Corby kept his head down and wouldn't smile, but she spun them both around and around.

"Dancing on the beach barefoot is the best," Maggie called out to everyone. Her linden tree necklace was swinging.

Maggie caught her dad's eye. He winked.

The frothy waves crashed on shore.

*BOOM shhhhhhh*

*BOOM shhhhhhh*

*BOOM shhhhhhh*

Forever.

# MAGGIE'S RECIPE FOR MOON MARSHMALLOWS

Lightly coat an 8-inch square pan with nonstick cooking spray and line with plastic wrap. Smooth out any wrinkles and spray wrap.

Whisk together ¾ **cup of confectioners' sugar** and ⅓ **cup cornstarch** in a medium bowl. Set aside.

In the bowl of an electric mixer whisk together **2½ envelopes powdered gelatin** with **1 cup cold water.**

In a small saucepan stir together ¾ **cup plus 2 tablespoons light corn syrup, 3 tablespoons honey, 1¾ cups granulated sugar** and ⅓ **cup water**.

Attach a candy thermometer to the side of the saucepan and set the saucepan on the stove on medium-high heat. Cook until the sugar reaches 245 degrees Fahrenheit, 6 to 8 minutes.

NOTE FROM MAGGIE: *Be very careful here, everybody. Here's where the sugar may pop out of the pan.*

Remove the saucepan from the heat and let cool to 225 degrees Fahrenheit, about 12 minutes.

Pour a stream of the sugar mixture into the electric mixer on low speed. When all the sugar mixture is added, increase the speed to medium-high. The mixture will get fluffy and thick.

After 5 minutes add **1 tablespoon vanilla extract** and **¾ teaspoon salt**. Continue mixing 15 minutes more until the marshmallow is very thick and the bowl feels cool.

With a rubber spatula fold in **finely grated zest of 3 lemons** or **¼ teaspoon more of vanilla extract**. For chocolate lovers, fold in ¼ **cup unsweetened cocoa powder**.

Scrape the marshmallow mixture onto the prepared baking pan and let sit at room temperature for 2 to 3 hours. Cut into squares, or use a cookie cutter and cut into circles or hearts.

Yummy yum! Moon Marshmallows!

This recipe was adapted from *The Craft of Baking* by Karen DeMasco and Mindy Fox. Clarkson Potter Publishers, New York, 2009.

# ACKNOWLEDGMENTS

Thank you first to my editors, Mary Kole, Amy Betz and Paula Cappa. You are wonders all, and I am so grateful for your expertise and help in making Maggie blossom.

Thank you to the fifth and sixth graders (now older!) at the Nantucket Lighthouse School in Nantucket for showing me all the cool secret spots by the beach and for giving me a starfish we spotted in the sand.

Thank you to the helpful naturalists at the Museum of Natural Science at the Nantucket Maria Mitchell Association, who seem to know every blade of beach grass on the island.

Thank you to the Nantucket commercial fishermen who sat me down and told me about your fishing days at sea and your dogs, several named Scupper. A scupper is a drain hole in the back of boats. Most of the fishermen wore backward base-ball caps, like Cap'n Hatch in my story.

Thank you to author Caroline Leavitt for your lively and creative suggestions with the earliest versions. They sparked my imagination.

Thank you to my poet friend, Carol Bell, for *ker-klunk.*

Thank you to wonderful Denise Alicea Mullinex for her quick, intuitive understanding of all things technical. I wouldn't have a book without you.

And thank you to all my beta readers, middle-graders and grown-ups, for your feedback from early drafts to final drafts. A special thanks to Betsey Brooks from Nantucket. Without you, Cap'n Hatch's golden lab, Scupper, would have been called Scutter and lost his true Nantucket spirit.

Thank you, and love to my daughter, Sarah, for her spontaneous phrase, "that salty, summer feeling." Like Maggie, she was nine years old when she said it while twirling on the beach.

To G. J., my son. Maggie's brother in the story, P. J., is named after you with love.

And last, but certainly not least, thanks to all of you wonderful people at Girl Friday Productions for holding my hand throughout the book production process and creating with me the most beautiful book.

A very special note to my readers: this book is dedicated to the Maggie in all of you. May you find your own kind of gumption and stand up to the Cap'n Hatches in your life.

# ABOUT THE AUTHOR

Cynthia Magriel Wetzler used to be a journalist and wrote many stories for The *New York Times*. She loved interviewing and writing about really interesting people. But she followed her dream and started writing children's stories so she could make up magical worlds with magical characters right out of her imagination. Maybe you might like to be a journalist or a writer someday? She has grown children and lives with her husband in northern Westchester County, New York. Their high-spirited little dog, Rodney, is the total inspiration for Blissful in this book. Here he is.

Follow Cynthia at www.witchymagicandmemaggie.com and www.writinglikeadancer.com.

Made in the USA
Coppell, TX
29 October 2020

40471296R00173